BAD DIAGNOSIS

THE WINSTON BROTHERS
BOOK TWO

DORI PULILTANO

Cover designed by Taylored Designs
Editor: Striding Ibis Editing

Author Dori Pulitano

First Printing: August 2022

READER

Warning

This is Book Two in the Winston Brothers Series.

Trigger Warning:
This book contains situations intended for adult audiences.
There are explicit sexual encounters, profanity, domestic
violence, rape, and death/murder.

If this is a potential trigger for you, I strongly
recommend you don't read it.

Quote

It's not a bad thing to fall in love...

— JUSTIN TIMBERLAKE

PROLOGUE

Gage

FAMILIAR SOUNDS THUNDER in the hallway outside my bedroom, jerking me out of bed. I've never known a time when my parents had a *normal* marriage. For the last few years, I've struggled to understand why she stays with him. Sure, we have a big house and more money than most, but at what price?

Even if he's my father, money hardly makes him a man. To me, and my brothers Drake and Roland, he's more like *Beelzebub*. Twisting the knob, I take a deep breath and step out from the safety that my room gives me, and into the cold and loveless hallway.

"Mom?" My veins fill with concern when I see my mother, huddled in a defensive position. Her body is dangerously close to a massive statue that fills the corner of the hallway. It's one of many ugly and ridiculously expensive art pieces my dad had to buy. Hearing her whimper can only mean one thing.

The old mans at it *again*.

"Gage, baby." Her voice sounds defeated as she calls out to me. "Go back to your room."

"Please, Mom. Come with me. My door locks." I motion for her to come inside with me—to lock out the monster who suddenly appears behind her like a demonic apparition.

"*Boy.*" His tone is bitter and filled with nothing but hatred as he narrows his beady eyes on me. "Mind your damn business and get the fuck out of mine. This is between your mother and me."

I straighten my shoulders and move to get in his face. "No. You're nothing but a bully. Why don't you just *leave?*"

The sting of the back of his hand makes me wince, but I stand firm, unwilling to leave my mother, whose mouth gapes in shock.

"What the hell?!? *Gage.*" My mother cries out. "Frank, stop it. He's your son, for Christ's sake."

"He'll learn not to interfere in grown-up matters. Won't you, boy?" He steps toward me, but my mother latches on to his arm.

The rage burning in my father's eyes as he turns toward her spurs me into motion. My mother grunts, her screams cut off as his fist connects with her jaw. I watch in horror as she falls to the ground, bones crunching as her head strikes the gaudy replica of the Aphrodite of Knidos statue. It lolls to the side as blood spurts out of the gaping wound, staining the usually pristine carpet beneath her. My father disappears into their room as she slumps to the floor, leaving me frozen in shock.

The sound of a door opening turns me around to find a scared and confused Roland standing there with his eyes wide as saucers. Drake steps out behind him and ushers

Roland back inside with him, leaving me to check on my mother. When I drop to my knees beside her, I know something is wrong.

"Mom." I shake her body, willing her to say something —*anything*. But she just stares at me with a vacant expression. "*Mom*. Please talk to me. *Please*."

My dad steps back into the hallway, and my vision blurs as he spits out. "You did this! *You* fucking did this."

"Gage?" My eyes widen when I see Drake standing in the open again. He stares at me with uncertainty, his eyes flicking to our mothers unmoving frame.

Shaking my head, I urge my younger brother, "Go back to your room, Drake. Lock the door and don't come out. For any reason. Do you understand me?"

His eyes remained locked on the still form of our mother. She's still bent in a crooked position against the wall, blood seeping into the cream threads beneath her head.

"*Mom?*" Drake calls outs, his bottom lip trembling with the crack in his voice as he says my name. "Gage?" The look he gives me guts me to the core.

"Drake." I speak his name, begging for him to turn around.

"This is your fault, Gage. You did this." Our father moves further into the hallway, a gun raised as he screams his vile hatred at me. "You killed your mother."

I push to my feet and point at him, my eyes narrowing as I see red. "No. *You* did that. You're a fucking monster."

"I'm your father." His voice rises as he lurches toward me. "I'll kill you for this, boy."

"Fuck you!" I cry out as I launch myself at him.

I'm done letting him treat us like this. My fingers wrap around the gun as we fall backwards and land on the floor. Pushing the gun away from my chest, I try to pull it free of his hold. Instead, a loud blast echoes through the narrow hallway and my father's body goes limp above me.

"Gage!" Drake kneels on the carpet, his knees squishing into the thick pile that's turning crimson, with the blood flowing freely from the left side of my father's chest. "Oh, God... please don't be dead." He cries, pulling the lifeless body off me.

"Drake." I turn my head toward him as I push to my knees. Drake's eyes are wide with shock, but when he hears me speak, he nods. "Call 9-1-1."

"He's dead," Drake mutters, his voice barely a whisper. "Dad's dead."

"Drake." I call his name again. "9-1-1."

"I thought..." Drake pushes to his feet as he stares down at the man we call our father.

I move toward my mother's still form. "I know, buddy. I know. But mom needs help, so go call 9-1-1." I watch as he makes the call. I faintly hear the operator's voice in the background, but all I can focus on is my mother.

Rolling her to her back carefully, I press my head against her chest. Not hearing any sounds to make me think she's breathing, I tilt her head back, worried I'm doing more damage than good. "Please mom... you have to be okay." I blow a breath into her mouth, willing the air into her lungs.

"One, two, three..." I count the beats as I press her chest. It feels like hours before someone is tapping my shoulder.

"Son, let me take over."

Crashing to my butt, I let the paramedic work on her. But as he does, I know it's too late—my mother is gone. Glancing to my side, I see my father's still form and I move without thinking. I'm on my feet, standing over his body. "You fucking deserved this, you bastard. But she didn't." I kick him, *hard.* I keep kicking him, years of anger billowing out of me with each blow of my foot. I don't stop until arms wrap around me and drag me from his side.

"Hey—stop. Whoa there, I got you." Tears burn trails of broken dreams down my face as I watch them load my mom onto the stretcher. "Can you tell me what happened?"

My eyes finally focus on the man still holding me back. "I killed him." I point to my father's lifeless body. "After he killed her..." I tip my head at the stretcher being hurried down the hallway, then add with a soft sob as I halfway motions to where Drake is standing with Roland at his side, "...and before he could kill *them.*"

"I have to take you in, son."

He's far gentler than he could be as he pulls my arms behind my back, but it's the cool metal that sobers me as he clicks the cuffs against my wrists. "You have the right to remain silent. Anything you say can and will be used against you in a court of law. You have a right to an attorney. If you cannot afford an attorney, one will be appointed for you. Do you understand your rights?"

I nod, words failing me as he leads me through the hall of my home. The murmurs of the other men don't go unnoticed by me. They're not surprised at the turn of events—not when they've been out here before. Only my dad is—was a smooth talker and *never* seemed to get caught. I suppose that's why we didn't have any people working her. Our gaudy, oversized house was left to us to take care of so no one would see the gilded cage we *actually* lived in.

"Hey," Drake screams, rushing toward us. "Where are you taking him?"

"It's standard procedure, son. In fact—" the surly man nods toward his partner. "—they all need to be brought in."

Drake cries out, trying to grab at me. "You're *arresting* him?"

"Drake." My calm voice snaps him out of the confusion, blinding him. "Get Roland. It's going to be okay, but you need to be there for him."

Drake glances around, the reality of what's happening hitting him hard. "Gage... what's going to happen now?"

"I don't know, buddy. I don't know."

I close my eyes and slide into the back of the patrol car, jerking when the door slams shut. The officer climbs in, turning his body toward me. "I know this is hard right now—but it will all work out."

"You don't know that. The only family I have is gone... what does that mean for them?" I tilt my head toward Drake and Roland, who are being led out by a uniformed officer. "If I go to jail... they go into the system."

The officer taps the steering wheel. "You aren't going to jail, young man. What you did was honorable—and not something a kid should ever have to do. I'm sorry you're being carted off like a common criminal, but it's standard—"

"Procedure. I know." I close my eyes and lean my head back against the seat.

At seventeen, I shouldn't be thinking about who is going to take care of my brothers. Especially Roland—he's only four and deserves a life that's not like this. I can't help but wonder if going into foster care would be best for him and Drake, but even thinking about it makes my heart clench.

We might not have been given the love we deserved from our parents, but the three of us share a bond that can't be broken. Not even by the monster who raised us.

The cruiser pulls into the parking lot, and I'm ushered into the precinct. Looks of pity meet my gaze from the receptionist that I'm hurried past, all the way to the rookie cop who pretends to type at his computer as he steals glances at me while I sit in the hard-backed chair for what feels like forever.

The cuffs are eventually taken off, but the damage is already done. Even though they keep saying I acted in self-defense, I stare down at my hands, seeing nothing but the dried blood that I can't escape. My mother's blood... and his blood. It's everywhere—my hands, my clothes, even dried to my face, which I can feel, but I thankfully can't see.

"Can I wash my hands, please?" My eyes flick to the officer standing guard.

He must see the panic in my eyes because his hardened expression softens. "Yeah—sorry, kid. We should have cleaned you up the minute you got here. Come on, I'll take you to the bathroom."

Following him, I close myself into the adjoining bathroom and brace my hands against the sink. Lifting my head, I stare at the reflection, looking back. Flicking the water on, I shove my palms beneath the flow. The water runs pink as the remnants of the night swirl and disappear down the drain. I pump soap into my hand and scrub my hands over my face, begging for the stain of what I did to wash off. My body tightens and I let out a sob as I scrape my skin raw.

Glancing up, I stare at the tear-stained eyes glaring back. Lashing out with my fist, I punch the glass. Over and over, my knuckles connect until a splinter appears. Hitting it harder, the glass splits, cutting into my knuckles as it crumbles to the floor. I stumble back away from the mirror and let out a horrendous sob. Sliding down to my butt, I scream, letting the sadness and rage wash over me.

"Hey." The officer steps inside. "Jesus, kid." He grabs some paper towels and presses them into my tattered hands. "Dispatch, I need a medic in the interrogation room." He presses his hand to my shoulder and forces me to look at him. "I know this is hard, kid. What you've grown up with is not normal. People who love each other don't put themselves, much less their kids, through that kind of violence. And you're not alone… there's someone here to get you and your brothers. I think she's going to be good for you guys. Maybe… just maybe, when this ordeal is over, you can try to have a normal life. Don't let darkness take you down. You hear me?"

I glance up at him and blink. "How am I supposed to have anything normal ever again? I killed my own father."

"No. You killed the man who created you. He wasn't a father, Gage."

Hearing my name from his lips makes me break a little more. "I have his blood. What if I turn out like him?"

"You don't let that happen. Make this life something good—show him what you can become despite the man he was. *In spite* of him."

I nod, letting him lift me to my feet and help me back into the interrogation room. An EMT is waiting for us. After he cleans up my knuckles and applies a few butterfly stitches, the officer hands me an oversized t-shirt emblazoned with 'Pig Roast - APD Annual Charity BBQ'. I shrug off my blood-smeared shirt and hand it to the EMT, who promptly dumps it into what looks like a trash bag, and tug it on, frowning that I'm practically swimming in it. But at least it isn't covered in blood. I'm taken to another room where my brothers are waiting.

"Gage." Drake launches himself into my arms and squeezes me like I'm going to disappear. "I thought I wouldn't see you again."

I hug him back. "I'm not going anywhere, buddy. Rol?" I open my arms, beckoning my four-year-old brother over. "I got you guys. It's going to be us from here on out, okay?"

"Okay." Drake sniffs against me. "But what about her?" He points to a woman sitting in a chair against the wall.

"Who's that?" I watch as she stands and moves toward us.

"Gage." She stops, unsure of how to proceed. "I'm Julie Winston, your aunt."

I step back, pulling Drake and Roland with me. If she's a Winston, she's going to be just like my father. "No." I stiffen with my brothers clutched in my arms. "We don't need you."

"I'm not like him, Gage. And I can't tell you how sorry I am for taking this long to save you boys. Had I—" Her voice cracks, but she clears her throat and straightens her spine.

"I'm here now. And I promise you, life will be nothing like what it was. I promise."

After listening to her and learning why we'd never met her, I agree to let her take custody of us. Knowing it's the only way I can keep us together, Julie might be the lesser of two evils. And maybe, just maybe, she'll be different. As we finish with the paperwork, I lace my fingers with Roland's hand and hold Drake against me as we follow Julie out of the station.

As we climb into her car, I make a silent promise to the heavens above... hoping my mother can hear me. My brothers and I will never feel this kind of pain again—from here on out, it's just going to be the three of us.

Love is the road straight to hell... and one I'll *never* be taking again.

1

Gage

Present Day

My feet pound against the pavement as I push myself along the trails. Running is one of the many ways I release stress, and today, it's necessary. Being one of the most sought-after orthopedic surgeons, work can become convoluted—especially when I'm forced to deal with the head of ortho. Technically, that job should've been mine and there are days, like today, when I regret turning down the position. Slowing to a jog, I ease to a stop and bend over, pressing my palms against my knees. Charles Peters—the half-rate wannabe they gave the job to—likes to needle me about my father, the man who most still remember, as the ruthless businessman his kid killed. And that kid was me. But ruthless doesn't even *begin* to cover it. They have *no* idea what kind of monster we lived with.

Pulling out the t-shirt tucked in my waistband, I wipe the sweat off my face and lean my head to the sky. I'm caught momentarily in a memory when my body jolts forward suddenly.

I turn to castigate the responsible party. "What the fu—" but words escape me. Standing in front of me is the most beautiful woman I've seen in a while. Her chestnut brown hair is tugged back into a sleek ponytail, showing off the exquisite shape of her face. She looks away quickly, but not before I glimpse her beautiful emerald eyes.

"Dios, soy una chica estúpida." *God, I'm such a stupid girl.* She presses her hands against her head and continues her tirade, not noticing that I'm staring at her. "Casi derribé a este hermoso hombre porque estaba ocupado mirando su cuerpo." *I nearly knocked this gorgeous man down because I was busy staring at his body.* Her arms wave around as she paces in front of me. Stopping, she glances at me, not really making eye contact, and bites down on her lip. "Y joder qué cuerpo es." *And fuck, what a body it is.* Her eyes follow my legs up as she appraises my body, her breath catching when she reaches my face and sees me smirking.

"You alright?" I smile, my own body threatening to expose just how much her beauty turns me on.

She blinks, her eyes widening when she realizes I witnessed her entire tirade. "Yes... But I should be asking you that. Are *you* okay?"

I tilt my head back and let out a laugh. "Sweetheart, it's going to take a lot more than a tiny thing like you to hurt me. Hell, it felt more like a butterfly ran into me, not—" I wave my hand over her body. "—someone like you."

"Someone like me?" She adjusts her stance, crossing her arms over her body.

Shaking my head. "You're taking my words wrong. How about we start over? I'm Gage Winston... and you are?"

I don't miss how she glances around before meeting my gaze again. Thrusting her hand forward, she says, "Poppy Jefferson."

"Well, Poppy Jefferson. Do you make it a habit to run over people in the park?"

She snorts, her body relaxing a bit. "No. Actually, I rarely come here. But today I managed to—" She pauses, as if not wanting to say what she almost did. "I, uh, found this place. You come here often?"

"Every day." I wipe my face again and smile. "I'm on my lunch break. I work over there." I point toward the direction the hospital is and grin.

"Oh." She blinks, following my finger's direction. "Must be nice to be so close to this beautiful sanctuary."

"It is... What about you, Poppy? What do you do?"

A weird expression crosses her face. "Nothing... My family is a bit—*protective*."

My eyes narrow, understanding dawning on me. "Do they know you're here?"

Poppy bites down on her lip, my eyes flicking towards the movement. "No. They think I'm having a spa day. Which I kind of am. Right?" She laughs. "My parents are dead, so my overprotective brother thinks he has to keep me under his thumb. To keep me from getting hurt."

"Jesus. This isn't the 1800s. How old are you, anyway?" I tug the shirt over my head, noticing how her eyes follow my movements and I hide my smirk under the fabric.

"Twenty-four." The smile she gives me is like a bolt of lightning to my chest and I mask the sharp breath with a forced cough. "What about you?" She tilts her head, appraising my frame.

Fuck. "Thirty-seven... an old man compared to you." This beautiful creature is beyond off limits at her young age.

"Puedo llamarte papi." *Can I call you Daddy?* she mumbles in Spanish before smiling up at me. "You're in pretty good shape for an old man."

Palming the back of my head, I scrunch my face and laugh. "Definitely well over thirty—but not an old man yet." Glancing down at my watch, I sigh. "As enlightening as this reminder of my slowly aging body has been, I need to get back to work. I still need to shower before the business of the day traps me."

"Well Gage Winston, fit old man... it was nice running into you—literally." She walks backwards, grinning. "Maybe I'll see you around again."

"I run every day—same time." I give her a knowing grin. "Oh, and Poppy?" I call out to her as she gets further away.

"Yeah?" she calls out.

"You can call me Daddy *anytime.*"

I turn, but not before catching her stumble from my words. I couldn't resist myself. Seeing as I'm fluent in three languages, her attempt to converse with herself about *me* didn't go unnoticed.

By the time I make it to my office, all I can think about is the woman. Despite our age difference, I'm drawn to her—which is crazy, since I swore off women for purposes other than sex. My father left a permanent scar on my soul, and I refuse to taint another human being with the darkness I still carry from him. Stripping off my shorts, I toss it into the basket I keep in my office and step into my private bathroom. Being the attending of orthopedics has its perks—case and point as I kick on the water and strip off my shorts.

Climbing beneath the spray, I press my hands against the cool tile and blow out a breath. Poppy seems to be at the forefront of my brain as visions of her swirl through my mind. Her eyes were the most captivating color I've ever seen. And I've seen plenty of eyes in my career as a doctor, but none the same shade of green as hers. In fact, I don't recall ever seeing green eyes quite this captivating. Her full, pouty lips held my attention as she spoke, and now, as I think back, I wonder if she found my staring creepy.

After rinsing the soap from my skin, I cut the water off and climb out. Dragging on a fresh pair of scrubs, I wander out of my office and head down to the ER. With six more hours left in my shift, I go in search of a cup of coffee, desperate to give myself a little kick-start.

The vibration in my pocket has me nearly spilling the cup of joe I just snagged. "Shit." Coffee spills over the rim, dotting the blue cotton on my thigh with brown. Sliding the device from my pants, I sigh.

"Drake," I mumble into the phone at my brother. He's five years younger than me but acts more like the older sibling. "This best be important enough to make me spill my coffee."

"Maybe you just need a sippy cup lid, brother." Drake chuckles at his own joke. "And anytime I call, it's important."

"Right... I take it court went well?" I roll my eyes as I set the cup down at the nurses' station and prop myself on the desk.

"Yep. That motherfucker had no leg to stand on when we showed the judge the photos of him buried balls deep in his mistress. His days of playing mental warfare on his wife and kids are over. He'll have supervised visitation for the next year."

"You really are a dick." I can't help but laugh at him. Drake is good at his job. Being a dick is a compliment of the highest order.

"It pays the bills—being a dick, that is."

"What's up? You lucked out and caught me in between busy spells. But..." I listen as he shuffles something in the background. "I have to head up to talk with some parents."

"Roland is in town in two days. We're going to see him. Clear your schedule."

"At least it's a Saturday. I was supposed to be on call in the ER, but I'll swap with Peterson."

"Good. I'll call you tonight with the details. Go break a leg." Drake laughs into the phone.

"Fuck you, Drake." One of the nurses stops in front of me. "Ugh, I have to go. Duty calls. But keep me posted—let's do dinner in the next day and come up with a game plan."

"Sounds good."

"Dr. Winston, I didn't mean to interrupt, but we have a patient who was just brought in. She might have a cheek fracture and Dr. Harris asked me to come grab you for a consult."

"Lead the way, Paula." I wave her on, following close behind her as we head toward one of the patient rooms.

We stop outside the closed door and Paula hands over the iPad. I scan the screen, a gasp escaping when I see the patient's name. *Poppy Jefferson* is in bold letters, mocking from behind the glass. Scanning the intake form, I see, she told the nurse she tripped and fell, hitting her face on the wooden banister at home.

Taking a calming breath, I close the folder and grip the knob in hand. Pushing open the door, I step inside. Poppy's eyes shoot up, shock that she quickly schools skitters across her swollen face. My blood fills with rage just seeing the damage to her beautiful skin, and I close my eyes and take a quick breath to get it under control. Opening my eyes, I turn my head to the burly man sitting in a chair beside her. He looks up from his phone and stands.

"Doctor." He moves to her side, and I don't miss the way her body tightens at his nearness. "I'm Carlos, a *close* friend of Ms. Jefferson."

"I see." I glance down at his hand and flick my eyes over to hers. "Mr. Perez, if you don't mind stepping outside while I assess the patient, I'd appreciate it."

He jerks back at my words. "I won't be leaving her side."

I step toward him and stop. "She has a right to patient confidentiality. And if you're not her husband, you'll need to wait outside. I can assure you, she's safe with me."

"*Please.*" Poppy looks at the man. "Just wait outside so I can get this over with."

He seems to study her for a moment before giving her a slight nod. "I'll be right outside in the hallway."

As soon as the door shuts, Poppy takes a breath and tries to force a smile. "So, this is where you work, huh?"

2

Poppy

HOW FUCKING HUMILIATING. The man I've been fantasizing about, the one I kicked myself for not getting a number from, is currently staring at me. Getting his number would have resulted in much worse than what currently has me sitting in front of the fine doctor—and I mean fine. I did my best to hide the recognition in my eyes, as it would only lead to suspicion and later a reminder of who owns me. My brother's handiwork landed me in the ER when he found out I skipped my spa appointment... again. I've been here more times than I can count, so it's shocking that this time, the man who's standing in front of me isn't a stranger—not really.

"So, those muscles aren't from being an orderly, huh?" I try to smile, but the pain hits me, and I take a sharp breath.

Gage moves to my side, his hands carefully sliding beneath my jaw as he tilts my face up. "Don't smile at me, Poppy. It could make your injuries worse."

Snorting softly, I mumble, "Tell me about it."

He shines a light in my eyes, making me blink. "Want to tell me what happened?"

"I already told the nurse." I flick my eyes away from his penetrating gaze, afraid he'll see the truth in them when I spew the well-rehearsed lies.

His thumb brushes the side of my face that isn't swollen. "Humor me."

My eyes meet his again and I nod. "I fell... you know I'm quite clumsy. Hell, I even bumped into a man today at the park while running."

"Is that so?" He smirks, his fingers gently probing the damage. "And what happened? Did you knock him on his ass?"

"A little ole thing like me?" I flutter my eyes as best I can, wincing through the pain. "Nah—I doubt I had any effect on him." I swallow my nerves. The weird banter between us bordering on flirtatious seems out of character for a man like him. Still, I can't take my eyes off his as he moves closer, adjusting his hands beneath my jaw in a tender hold.

He pauses his assessment, my face cupped in his palms. "I'm sure you affected him more than you think. Now... your face. How did this happen?"

Closing my eyes, I force out the practiced words. "I tripped and lost my footing as I was heading up the steps—I needed a shower after my run in the park this morning. Unfortunately, I miscalculated the step's distance and didn't plant my foot correctly. The damn banister did not cradle my fall like the gentleman from this morning."

Gage's lips quirk as his eyes shine with mirth at my innuendo of our encounter this morning. "Doubt the banister realized it had a beautiful woman crashing into it. Alright…" He lets go of my face and steps to the computer hanging on the wall. "I'm going to send you up for a CT scan. I need to make sure you didn't damage the orbital bone, or that there are any fractures in your cheek."

"Okay." I lean back on the bed and blow out a breath in frustration. "How long will this take? I should call my brother—he's probably worried."

Gage turns to glance at me over his shoulder and I see the way his brow quirks. "Why? Your boyfriend seems capable of ensuring you get the proper care."

"He's a bit of a control freak and demanded I keep him informed of the outcome." I avoid his 'boyfriend' comment and turn my head away from him, careful not to bump my cheek on the side of the bed.

Gage moves back beside me. "Turn this way, Poppy. I need to stitch the cut, or you'll risk having an ugly scar."

Tears well in my eyes and threaten to fall as I lean my head towards him. "What… afraid I'll look like Leatherface?" I try to find humor in a situation that is making both of us uncomfortable.

His gaze softens as he sets the needed materials on the table beside my bed. "Even with a tiny scar, that would be impossible, Ms. Jefferson. But… I will do everything I can to make sure it doesn't. In fact—" he sets down the needle and steps to the door. I watch as he calls the nurse into the room. "—Paula, can you call Dr. Brooks? I'd like him to come down here and suture Ms. Jefferson's wound, so we ensure minimal scaring on her face."

"You want the head of plastics?" Paula glances between us, a look of confusion written across her features.

"Yes." Gage scowls at her, making her cower slightly. "Jack owes me a favor. Let him know this is me cashing in."

"Yes, sir." She darts out of the room, tugging the door closed behind her.

"That… that's unnecessary." I stare at Gage. "I'm sure you can stitch me up, Dr. Winston."

He sits down on the bed beside me, reaching out and cradling my uninjured cheek in his palm. His touch is gentle, giving a weird sense of comfort, which has me leaning into him. "That may be true… but I want to make sure you have the best—*Poppy*."

"Oh…" My voice comes out as a whisper. Gage's hand doesn't immediately drop, and we're caught in this weird trance until the door opens and a man, I assume the head of plastics, steps inside.

He glances at our precarious position, causing Gage to drop his hand from my face, and stand. "Brooks, glad you could grace us in the ER."

"Well… I was told you were cashing in my IOU. And since you're not a man that does that… I was curious to see what made you do it." His eyebrow quirks as he smirks at Gage. "Now, I understand."

Gage grumbles something under his breath as he steps back. "Just stitch her face—let's not make this a big deal, okay?"

He nods and moves beside the bed. "I'm Dr. Brooks. You're going to feel a slight pinch and burn, but it will be less than what it would be if I stitched you without it. Okay?"

"Okay." I tilt my face to the side, the pinch of the needle making me tense and my eyes water. I feel a slight pull, but before I realize it, he's done with the sutures.

"All done, pretty girl. These will dissolve on their own. If you shower, pat them dry when you get out—otherwise, there's no need to follow up with me. Unless, of course, you have issues."

"Thanks Jack." Gage shakes his hand and closes the door as Dr. Brooks leaves. "The x-ray tech is here to take you upstairs. I'll be back once you're done." Gage steps out, making way for a man in scrubs pushing a wheelchair.

"Think you can sit in this, or do I need to push you in the bed?" He nods to the chair in front of him.

Sliding my feet to the floor, I amble over to him and plop down. "I can manage."

As we move into the hallway, Carlos steps beside me. "Where are you taking her?"

"For a CT. We'll be back in about thirty minutes." The male tech responds as he moves me down the hallway. "Hey." He turns his head, stopping Carlos in his tracks. "You can't come with. Wait in her room."

Carlos puffs up, trying to intimidate the man, but I interrupt. "Carlos... please don't embarrass me. Just wait in my fucking room."

He glares at me, but reluctantly turns and heads back. "That your boyfriend?"

"God no... the boyfriend, or so he likes to call himself, is worse than that moron. Be glad he didn't come with me. I know I am. I fucking hate him, too."

The tech snorts. "Then why you with him?"

I shrug, wishing I could just walk away from all of them. "It's complicated."

"Usually is." He pushes me through a set of double doors into a cold room. "Alright, little lady. Hop up there and lay back."

He gets me situated. "Just lay still. This won't take long."

I lay there, staring at the inside of the metal machine. How the hell did I get myself into this fucking nightmare I call my life? Oh—I know how. My brother—rather, stepbrother—is a fucking lunatic. When my mom married his father, I knew it was too good to be true. When *he* died, Alessandro's true colors showed. At first, he tried to say I belonged to *him*, but I fought him tooth and nail. So, he did the next best thing... he gave me to Eduardo, his right-hand man.

Property is exactly how he views me and treats me. That's a lie. He treats his property better. My eyes close and I can't help thinking of my mother.

Then my mom was killed in a car accident, and I had to face the truth. My life was no longer my own. Locked in a fortress of hell, I'm expected to do whatever my *big* brother or his monster of a friend demands. How I've held on to my virginity is short of a miracle. It's the one thing Alessandro demands of Eduardo. I'm not to be touched like that until we are married, which is sometime this year.

"Alright sweetie, we're done."

My eyes snap open to find the kind eyes of the tech. He helps me into the chair and carts me back down to my room. My guard dog, Carlos, is waiting inside my room and stands when we push inside.

"Well?" He glares at the tech, who snorts in return.

"It takes time for the scans to be read. You might as well get comfortable—you'll be here a while. As for you." He tugs the blanket over my legs with a cheery smile. "Push the button if you need anything."

Once I'm alone with him, he startles me by moving beside me and grabbing my chin. The pain is almost too much and my eyes well with tears. "Listen here, puta. You best not say anything to anyone about what happened. Because if you do, this will look like child's play. You got me?"

He shoves my face away and I nod, tears welling in my eyes again. "I didn't say anything, Carlos."

The door opens and Gages steps through, holding a tablet in his hands. His eyes narrow on my face and Carlos' proximity to the bed. "Everything okay in here?"

"Yes." Carlos turns to me. "Recuerda lo que dije." *Remember what I said.*

He obviously thinks Gage doesn't know what he's saying, but as my eyes flick to the man glowering at the foot of the bed, I silently plead with my eyes for him to keep his ability to speak the language to himself.

I watch as understanding dawns in his eyes and he gives me a slight nod. "I'm sorry. I don't speak Spanish." He glances over at Carlos. "What did you say?"

"Oh." Carlos chuckles. "I just told her we would leave soon."

"I see." Gage looks at me and I swear the temperature in the room drops. "He's right. Your scans came back and you're lucky, Ms. Jefferson. No fracture. You'll just sport one hell of a shiner for a while. I suggest you take it easy for a few days."

He pauses, holding my gaze. "That means no exercise, Ms. Jefferson. Besides the stitches you have earned, you also have a mild concussion. And jostling will agitate the injury. Now." Gage taps the screen in his clutch. "A nurse will be in to get you discharged. Follow up with your primary care physician in a few days if you experience severe headaches that can't be tamed with over-the-counter medication."

"Dr. Winston," I call out as he turns to leave. "Does this mean no running for me?"

His head swivels between Carlos and mine, but I can see the hint of a smile beneath the false expression he's masking it with. "Yes, Ms. Jefferson. Especially running." He starts toward the door but pauses at the entrance. "I'm sure once you're healed, the trails will be exactly as you left them."

With that, he disappears out of my room, leaving me with Carlos. My eyes drift from the closed door over to where he sits, and I am relieved to find him engrossed in something on his phone. I close my eyes and for a moment allow myself to think about what it would be like to be free of my stepbrother and Eduardo—and maybe with someone like Dr. Gage Winston. I imagine a man like him treats women with dignity and respect. Something I don't get, currently. If the throb in my cheek isn't reminder enough, the constant control is.

"Wake up." Carlos slaps my foot. "Press the fucking button— I want to get out of here."

And just like that, my solitude is gone.

One day I'll get away from them... even if it's in a pine box.

3

Gage

STARING down at the little boy who looks like he's seconds away from a melt-down, I tug my stethoscope off and dangle it in front of him.

"How about *you* listen to my heart while I look at your foot?"

His big brown eyes pan up to meet my gaze and I can't help but see Roland in him. "Listen to your heart?"

I smile. "Yes. I've been told I don't have one, so maybe you can check and give me a second opinion."

I get a giggle out of him as he lifts the round end and presses it against my chest. While he's preoccupied, I gently grip his foot and begin assessing the damage. Apparently, his older brother was backing out of their driveway, and Billy, the one currently listening for the beat of my non-existent heart, ran out to tell him goodbye. It could have been much worse, but fortunately, Billy was knocked to the side of the car when his brother hit reverse. Unfortunately, his left foot wasn't as lucky, and the rear tire used his ankle like a speed bump. The seventeen-year-old brother heard his scream and had enough sense to call 9-1-1 instead of trying to move him alone.

The paramedics brought in two hysterical kids. "Billy... Alex." A woman rushes into the room, her face pinched in concern.

"Mom." Alex stands, his body shaken with tears as his mother wraps him in an embrace. "I didn't mean to hit him —I didn't see him. He just—came out of *nowhere*."

"Shhh... Alex. It was an accident." She moves to the side of the bed, her eyes red with tears. "How's my baby?"

"Be quiet, mom. I'm listening for a heart," Billy whispers as he leans into my body, searching for the thumping sound.

Her eyes cut to me, and I shrug. "He was a tad freaked out. I've given him something for pain—which is why he seems pliable. The stethoscope was a distraction, so I could examine him. I'm Dr. Winston, by the way." I stand, pulling the stethoscope to drop out of Billy's hand and causing him to grunt in displeasure.

"Thank you, Doctor. How is he?" She reaches out and strokes his hair.

Keying in the order for an x-ray, I glance up and smile. "I think he's lucky. This could have been much worse—for both of them. Alex's quick reflexes and mindfulness to stop the car kept him from being hit twice. I think it's just a simple fracture, but I won't know for sure until he goes up for x-rays."

"Thank God." Alex sits down on the bed and ruffles his brother's hair as his mother pulls him against her side. "I don't know what I would do if something happened to either of my boys. They're all I have." She smiles adoringly at the boys before turning back to me. "Will he have to stay overnight?"

"Probably not. Unless the fracture needs surgery, I don't see why you can't go home tonight. If you'll excuse me, I need to check on some other patients. I'll be back once his scans are ready. A nurse will be down to take him to radiology soon."

The door shuts behind me and I amble my way over to the nurse's station. After giving Paula the specifics, I head up to my office. This week has been pure hell in the ER, and I am grateful for a day off—only three more hours to go.

I barely manage to sit down at my desk when a knock sounds at my door. "Enter."

My brother Drake steps through the door. "Hope I'm not catching you at a bad time."

"Did I miss a call from you?" I sit up straighter in my chair, concerned something is wrong.

Drake plops down across from me and shakes his head. "It's about Roland."

"Fuck. I knew this visit couldn't be about something good. What is it now?"

Drake sighs, pinching the bridge of his nose. "That mess with the tabloid from last year is blowing up again—except they've added a spin to it."

"I saw the photo, but what is it that has the gossip whores so fixated on *this* one?" I lean back in my seat.

Drake fishes out his phone and slides it across my desk. My eyes bug out of my head when I see the newest picture glaring back at me. "What the fuck?"

"Right?" Drake grabs his device and pockets it. "I knew he was into the lifestyle… but like *that?*"

My gut immediately coils, and I think back to growing up with my father. "Do you think it's because of all the shit he saw?"

"I don't know, Gage. Are you into the things you're into because of our father?" Drake glares at me. "I mean… I do it because I feel a sense of control—not because I like to…" He waves his hand and points toward his phone. "Do… *that.*"

"Have you talked to him?" I tap my fingers across the desk's smooth surface.

Drake shakes his head. "And say what? I don't think our little brother intended for that to get out. I suspect whoever took it did so without consent. It doesn't matter, though. It's done and now he's trying to salvage his image… *again.*"

I scrub my palm down my face. "If you aren't going to call him, then why are you here?"

Drake smirks at me as he leans forward. "Well, big brother. He isn't the only one in the gossip headlines." He slaps a folded paper on my desk. "*We* are mentioned as well. They seem to think that it's a family trait."

Tearing the paper open, I growl and ball it up. "Fuckers are just reaching."

"Are they? You and I like to dabble in the proclivities from time to time." He leans back in the chair and sighs. "I guess I'm just warning you to be careful. I plan to be extra cautious if I go to the club until this shit dies down. Hopefully, the label can spin this—or erase this from society's mind. Roland has worked too hard to have his dreams crash now. I've asked

Brian to look into things. If we need to sue the tabloid for defamation, we will."

"Defamation? How can you claim that when it's very obvious who's in the photo? But you do your thing... maybe this will die down and a lawsuit won't be necessary."

"We can hope." Drake pushes to a stand and moves toward the door. "Drinks this weekend?"

"Yeah... it's been a long week." I wave him off as he pulls the door closed behind him, leaving me alone with my thoughts.

We all dabble in a little BDSM, well... Drake and I do. That photo of my baby brother tells me he does more than dabble. When the three of us swore off involving our hearts by getting involved with relationships, we fell into the lifestyle. It allows us the ability to fuck with no strings. Thinking of fucking, my mind flashes to Poppy. It's been a week since I ran into her at the park—then here in my ER. I don't for a second believe she fell, not after seeing her chart. Poppy has been in the ER a total of sixteen times over the course of six months. Somehow, she's avoided being reported to the authorities, making me question the ethics of the people I work with. There is something peculiar about her situation, and I'm not able to put my finger on it.

The phone on my desk rings, ending any thought I have of the woman who seems to take up more space in my head than I care for. "Dr. Winston."

"Doctor, they're calling for you in the ER." Paula, the charge nurse's voice, comes through the line.

Grumbling, I push up from my chair. "I'll be right down."

The clock on the wall says there's only one hour left in my work week, making me thankful for the two days I'll have off.

As soon as I step out of the elevator, I know any plans I have for a relaxing night are shot to shit—the emergency room is a flurry of activity. The fire department is gathered at the nurse's station, watching as one of their own is worked on inside one of the rooms. My years of training kick in, and I run toward the fray.

"What happened?" I step inside the tiny room, muscling my way toward the firefighter a resident doctor straddles, pumping his chest.

"A warehouse fire. The roof caved in, trapping this guy and his partner."

"Partner?" I say, scanning the nearby rooms for another injured man.

My eyes connect with a nurse, whose gaze is glassy as she shakes her head. "Fuck," I mumble, "move." I push the young doctor off the firefighter and take over. "Paddles." I scream, covering his chest with the metal pads. "Clear." The room stills as the defibrillator shocks his chest. "Get the fucking head of cardio down here *now*."

The resident pushes epi, and I charge the paddles again. This time, when the machine sends a bolt of electricity into his chest, the sound of a rhythm fills the room. "What do we have?" The voice of Max Sheffield, head of cardio, fills the room.

"Thirty-year-old male. He was a firefighter on the scene of a warehouse fire. The roof collapsed, crushing him and his partner. Once the victim was dug out from under the remains of the building, paramedics noted fractures to his right tibia. Paramedics on-scene advised us they lost the victim's pulse en route to the ER."

"His name," I growl, interrupting the nurse who is speaking.

"I'm sorry…" she stutters.

I turn toward her, my temper ready to explode. "This man is a hero. We will stop referring to him as a victim and by his name. Do you see those men out there?" I point to the solemn men watching as we work on their partner. "They've already lost one member of their team. We're going to stop looking at this man as just another victim and as one of our own."

"Michael Fraser, sir."

"Thank you." I turn to Max. "What do you need?"

"A full workup. He has a pulse, but it's not great. And from the looks of that mangled leg—he needs to be in an OR yesterday."

Moving to his lower extremity, I close my eyes and center myself. Max is right. This man is going to be lucky to keep his leg. And the longer it takes to get him up to the OR, my chances of increasing his odds diminish.

"Can we take him now?" I narrow my eyes at Max.

He glances at Fraser and then out at the men with hopeful gazes. "I'll make it work. Two birds, one stone. Let's go."

We get him packed up as best we can and move into the hallway. One of the men from his station grabs my arm. "Will he —" He pauses, his voice hitching.

"I will do everything I can to bring your friend back to you, but time is ticking, sir. I'm sorry for your loss tonight—but I can't let it become two. I *won't*. Now… excuse me."

The men stare at us as we move around the corner and disappear through another set of doors. "You think he'll make it through surgery?" I glance at Max.

Max shrugs his shoulders. "Won't know until we get a CT. They're meeting me in there with the portable machine. It's been a while since we've worked in an OR together—wish it wasn't for this, though."

"Yeah. Me either. Seems the people who give everything to others are the ones who lose the most." We make it into the OR just as he codes again.

Max goes into hero mode himself, and as we work in tandem —we pull a miracle out of our asses. How he didn't die on the table or lose his leg is between him and God, because for a minute there, I was pretty sure it was going to be a choice between his life or the leg. Somehow, he survived the OR with both intact.

Once he's moved to ICU, I make the trek down to the waiting room. As I step through the double doors, a room of men and women who wear his station number stands, looking at me with fearful expressions. They've already had to deal with the loss of one, so their worry is warranted.

"Did he make it?" A burly man steps forward, his eyes taking in the blood-stained scrubs I'm wearing. I take a moment to look at him and notice his insignia identify him as the captain.

"Captain. I'm pleased to report that Firefighter Fraser pulled through surgery." A resounding cheer goes through the waiting room. The captain grabs my hand, shaking it wildly. "Now I know that's good news, but he's going to have a long recovery. The nurses are getting him set up in the ICU.

Someone will come get you when you can go see him. Is his family here?"

"We are his family." A female dressed in the familiar paramedic uniform steps forward. "I'm Gabby Holloway—the paramedic who brought him here, and his teammate. Michael doesn't have any family locally, but we called his brother, who will be here in the morning. Their parents have passed, so it's just them."

"Good. Well, when he arrives, have the nurse call me. I'll be happy to explain what we did and what to expect."

"Thank you, Doctor."

Gabby turns to the captain and hugs him. After a few handshakes and pats on the back, I slink away to my office and collapse in my chair. What was supposed to be one more hour of work turned into ten. It's nearly three in the morning and I'm debating whether to sleep here or tote my ass home. After debating, I decide the couch in my office won't do and trudge through the hospital to the parking garage.

Climbing into my SUV, I crank the engine and head away from the hospital. I think I might sleep for the day and a half I have off—at my age, these long hours are starting to kick my ass.

4

———

Gage

DESPITE KNOWING I shouldn't be here, the need to let off steam finds me at Club Polaris. It's been a little over two months since I've traipsed through the doors here, but the familiar sounds of gratification, paired with the deep burgundy of the walls, relax me more than I've been in a while. Unlike Drake, who seeks to dominate, I prefer the art of using rope during sex. Nothing gets me harder than seeing a woman completely bare beneath the woven threads I've knotted around her body as she suspends above the floor. Truth be told, I need to take my mind off a curvy woman who has taken up way too much residency in my head.

"Gage." A familiar face greets me as I sidle up to the bar. "Haven't seen you in here in a while. Wondered if you'd given up your pastime."

"Chris, you know how it is… work keeps me busy." I fist the glass of whiskey he's pressed in front of me and adjust the mask covering part of my face.

The employees here know every patron, but that's as far as our identity goes. Anonymity is paramount here for many reasons, but mostly because the members are wealthy. I imagine if it got out that the Chief of Police was into BDSM, he'd be persecuted without a second thought. Yeah... I know who he is, just as he knows who I am. The Chief wanted to learn the art of Shibari, and I'm considered a master rigger, so I volunteered to educate him in the ways of rope play.

He taps the bar and grins. "Ah, that's right—the life of a world-famous doctor. A few of your regulars have been asking for you. They'll be glad to see you're here tonight."

Dipping my chin, I stand. "Then I shouldn't keep them waiting."

It doesn't take me long to wind my way through the bodies filling the lounge. There are no rules at the club, other than everything must be consensual. Which explains the couple currently fucking on the black leather couch. They're regulars and seem to get a thrill from being out in the open. I don't care what people's kinks are, fucking is just that—fucking. This place gives my brothers and me the outlet we need to satisfy... well, our *needs*.

The room is just as I remember it. A massive bed sits at the center of the space. Above it, metal eyes are bolted into the ceiling. I brush my fingers over the metal fasteners protruding from the wall that provides the rigger options for binding the bunny. I chuckle to myself. *Bunny* is such a funny term for the woman being restrained. It makes me feel like a hunter catching my prey.

Moving toward the long dresser pressed against the far wall, I kick off my shoes and socks, setting them on top. As I'm removing my shirt, the sound of creaking has me glancing over my shoulder. A woman dressed in a black leather bustier and matching thong closes the door behind herself. Her body is thinner than I like, but tonight I don't care. I need to get off and her asshole will do fine.

She takes a few steps into the room and pauses. "Do you already have a bunny for the night?"

"No." I toss my shirt on the dresser and pull open the drawer. "Get undressed and stand by the bed." Gathering the needed supplies, I spin on my heel to face the woman.

Pleased to see she's followed my directions, I say, "Good girl." I slowly stalk toward her. I want to use the bed for what I have planned—what I need. I have no interest in suspension. My craving tonight is for the bunny to relinquish ultimate control.

"What's your safe word?" My fingertips smooth across her shoulder as I drag them down her arm.

"Purple." She whispers, her eyes still turned down toward the floor. While I don't partake in the various proclivities of BDSM, the women recognize even a rigger as their Dom.

My fingers wrap around her wrist, and I drag the arm behind her. "Give me your other arm."

She stretches her arm back, and I grab hold, pressing her arms together. Her body is pliable, giving me one hundred percent control of her movements. Using one hand, I pin her arms together and withdraw the hemp rope I shoved in my pocket. The room is silent except for the sound of her relaxed breaths.

"Hold your arms still."

My fingers command the twine as I wrap her wrists. The hemp fibers are smooth beneath my touch as I thread the line over and under, braiding them together around her creamy flesh. I slide the length of the material over her shoulder and step around her front. Draping the ribbon across her bosom, I wrap it around her side—repeating the process on the other side, until I have her chest tied the way I want it. I brush the dark strands of her hair out of the way and loop the rope under the artistic knots pressing against her back. My hand slips between her legs, my knuckles grazing her wet center. Her quick intake of breath tells me she's sensitive to the touch. Hell, even without the sound, I know what she wants —her pussy is dripping wet.

I make quick work of the remaining length and ease her onto the bed. Her chest presses into the bed as I position her onto her stomach and tug at her hips so she's in a downward dog position. The sight of her has my cock pulsing against my jeans, demanding to be set free and buried in her tight hole.

My palm connects against the globe of her ass, making her hiss. She wiggles her backside as she tries to rub her thighs together. No doubt she's trying to quell the burning need between her legs. "How do you feel, bunny?"

Her moan tells me what I need to know, so I step back and remove a condom from my pocket. After shucking my jeans, I step behind her and tug on the ropes holding her still. "Are you ready for me, bunny?"

"Yes... please, *sir*."

I rip the foil packet with my teeth and sheath my dick with the slick barrier. "Please what, bunny?"

"Fuck me." She groans as she pushes her ass into the air, causing her legs to spread slightly.

The sight of her slit glistening with moisture draws me in like a moth to a flame. Gripping her hips, I dig my fingers into her hips and bury my fingers into her core. As much as I want to lean forward and swipe my tongue through the shimmering honey, I don't. Two times I've broken my own rule and devoured a woman's pussy, but it's something I restrict myself from. For me, it feels too intimate—too… binding. I push my digits into her, hammering against her backside as I drive her body forward from the force.

Her mewls are like gasoline to the fire spreading through my veins. Needing more, I pull my hand from between her legs and smear the cream coating my knuckles around her puckered hole. She inches forward slightly, and I momentarily freeze, wondering if this is a hard limit for her. Another rule I've set for myself is only taking them there. It's not that I'm secretly gay… I just feel it's too risky. I don't want to bind myself to a woman ever. Risking an accidental pregnancy is not a game I want to play. Most are accepting of that here, but there were two times I fucked up, nearly costing me everything.

"Is this—" I trace the rim of her backside. "A hard limit?" My thumb presses against the opening slightly, waiting for her response. When she pushes into me, causing the pad of my finger to slide inside, I smile. "Good girl. Do you want me to stick my cock in here?"

"Please." She practically growls her answer, shoving her ass into me harder.

Pulling my hand from her backside, I use my palms to separate her cheeks and spit into the hole, clenching with anticipation. Fisting my shaft, I press the tip against her opening and grip her hips. "Hang on, *bunny*, this is going to be rough."

I slam into her, not giving her any time to adjust to my size. I've been blessed by the cock gods, so I know I'm probably ripping her in two. And that thought only drives me wild. Easing out and slamming back into her, she moans louder.

Tugging against the binds, I use the ropes like a bridle and ride her like a horse. She's confined to this position, making me the ultimate master of her body. The sensations of her orgasm flutter around my cock as she cries out, her walls exploding in ecstasy around me. Needing this to last, I withdraw and rip the condom off my dick and toss it to the floor.

I flip her over and climb onto the bed. My body straddles hers, placing my steel-hard member in her face. Using my brute strength, I pull her up, pressing her body against the headboard. "Suck me off."

My fingers tangle into her hair as she opens her jaw and takes me into her mouth. The feeling of her lips wrapped around me sent a trickle of electricity across my skin. I can't stop my hips from bucking. "*Bunny.*" I growl a warning. "Don't gag on my cock. Swallow it all and show me how much you like it when you take it deep in that throat of yours."

The vibration of her moan causes me to close my eyes and hiss. She moves her head along my length and I can feel the impending orgasm build. "Harder, bunny." I tighten my grasp on her hair, pushing her down on my dick. Her lips clamp down harder, putting more pressure against the throbbing vein that runs from my balls to the tip. It's the trigger I need.

My balls tighten and I throw my head back, closing my eyes as the eruption begins. Cum spurts out in hot ribbons, filling her cheeks. She gulps me down, never breaking the seal of her mouth around my cock. When the last drop is sucked dry, she releases my shaft.

I let go of her hair and climb off the bed. Immediately, I roll her over and begin removing the ropes from her body. She lays still, allowing me to slip the hemp ribbons off, a process that takes time so as not to damage her flesh any more than it is. While the knotting is not tight, the ropes will leave a slight redness where she was wrapped. Once the last piece of twine has been taken off, I wind the material up and walk it to the dresser.

"Stay there," I command her to wait.

As instructed, she waits for me to return. I never leave my rope bottom to tend to their own skin after a session. Squeezing some lotion into my hands, I warm the liquid first, then place my hands on her back. She is stoically still as I rub the cream into her back, tracing the reddened lines that mar her skin. They'll fade, leaving no lasting scar, but the doctor in me needs to do this for her.

Once I finish, I grab my discarded pants and boxers, pulling them on. I place the lotion and rope back into the dresser and slip my shirt on. When I turn, I find the room is void of the brunette I just used for my own pleasure. Though it was the first time binding her, it was obviously not her first rodeo. Good subs knew their role—be seen, be used, be quiet.

Leaving the club, I thought I'd feel better. But a restlessness still plagues me. I'm not sure why I still feel off-kilter, but even expelling the energy wrapped around my chest like a vice hasn't lessened it much. Glancing at my phone, I sigh. It's a little after eleven pm and I'm not even remotely tired. It's going to be a long night.

5

Gage

I'VE BEEN on shift for three hours and I want to strangle the ER staff working with me today. Between the attending physician Harvey Olsen and me, we've been run ragged because of the massive pile-up on 285. Fucking truck drivers and their inability to maintain their lanes is a normal occurrence in Atlanta traffic. But that isn't the issue. The issue is the incompetence of the nurses on staff. More than once, they've failed to discharge a patient in a timely manner, and worse, they left one in radiology.

"If you can't get your shit together, I'm going to have Callie send you home. Do I make myself clear, Ashley? If you're too distracted by whatever is going on in your personal life, you don't need to be here."

I turn and start toward the front when the sound of my name being called halts my movement. Spinning on my heel, I find paramedics rolling in with a patient. Dr. Olsen waves me over. "I need you to look at this break." He grunts as he wheels the gurney into the tiny room.

I push around the firefighter, assisting with moving the woman to the emergency room bed. I'm not prepared to see that the patient is Poppy. *"Poppy."*

"You know her?" The paramedic glanced between us. "We got the call that someone had fallen down a flight of stairs. When we arrived on the scene, Ms. Jefferson was at the base of the stairs, unconscious. Upon assessment, we established vitals were slightly elevated, but normal. The major concern was—"

"Her wrist." The sight of her mangled wrist twists the insides of my gut—not to mention an obvious deformity of her collarbone. She's lucky she's not dead based on the impact she must've achieved when landing. "And I am assuming her skull." I turn to Olsen who is typing something into the iPad he cradles. "Olsen, I need her taken to CT, *again*. Has she regained consciousness at all?" I turn toward the paramedic, who shakes his head.

"Not really. She mumbled something about gauges, but it made no sense to any of us. Honestly, I worry she's got a severe head injury we aren't seeing."

Pushing aside the knowledge she was likely saying my name —knowing she was coming here, perhaps—I nod. "Yeah, me too. This isn't her first fall. As you can see, her face still hasn't healed from her visit here a few weeks ago."

My jaw clenches as I brush her hair from her face and examine the previous injury. "Who was with her when you arrived?"

"Two males. I think maybe one was her brother—I don't remember. I'll go grab the chart again." The female paramedic excuses herself to retrieve the electronic tablet she'd set down on the nurse's station.

I'm about to follow the paramedic out, needing answers, when the sweetest sound stops me. "I slipped in some water. Am I in the hospital again?"

Turning, I find Poppy fluttering her eyes open. She winces when she attempts to sit up, muttering a swear word under her breath. "*Fuck.*"

"Ms. Jefferson, please don't move. I was just about to take you up to CT." I lean down so my lips are close to her ear. "Please, Poppy, it's Gage. Tell me what really happened. You and I both know this wasn't because you slipped in water. Is someone hurting you?"

She holds my gaze, and I can see the internal battle waging war inside her head. Just as her lips part to answer with what I'm certain is the truth, the sound of a furious person causes her to snap her mouth closed.

"Where is she?!?" A male's voice echoes through the hallway.

Dr. Olsen gives me a sympathetic glance before turning to look at the man making his way toward the room.

"Well... doesn't look like we're going to need to wait on the medic to come back with a name." He steps aside. "Sir? Are you here for Ms. Jefferson?"

I don't recognize him as the man from the earlier incident, and I can't help but narrow my gaze at him. "Care to explain how she wound up like this... *again?*"

"She slipped in water." He cuts his eyes toward Poppy, and I don't miss the way he glares at her. "Poppy is quite clumsy. She wasn't paying attention and spilled her glass, slipping in her own mess. I heard her scream, but by the time I made it into the foyer, she was already at the bottom of the steps. I called 9-1-1 right away."

Even I can tell his response is rehearsed. I've seen it enough times to know he's covering either for himself or a friend. Glancing back at Poppy, I see she's fallen back asleep. "She needs to be evaluated by a specialist to ensure she doesn't have a life-threatening concussion. Do me a favor, don't let her stay asleep. I'll be back in a few. Dr. Olsen, can you manage?"

He gives me a nod as I step around him and quickly dart into the on-call room. Something isn't right, and I desperately need answers. Pulling my phone from the pocket of my scrubs, I swipe to open the screen and scroll to Drake's contact.

"What's up, big brother?" Drake answers on the first ring.

"You in court?" I grit my teeth, trying to quell the anger boiling inside me.

"Nope. Something wrong?"

"Kind of. Look, I had a woman come into the ER with a likely broken collarbone and right wrist. She claims it was from slipping on spilled water, but..." my voice trails off. I don't have to say it out loud for Drake to read the underlying concern. He's dealt with this shit almost as much as I have in his line of work.

I hear the frustrated sigh through the phone. "You think it's domestic violence?"

"I do. But when I pressed the matter, she clammed up and wouldn't answer any more questions." Groaning, I take a deep breath. "Then her husband or boyfriend showed up and I couldn't press anymore."

"You want me to do some digging?"

"Not yet. But I'm going to send you her information. Will you just keep an ear to the ground? Let me know if you hear something?"

"Yeah. Gage?" There's a slight pause. "Is there something I need to know about this woman? Do you know her or something?"

I mumble into the phone and huff. "Or something." I hear the paging system go off, calling for a doctor to the ER. A multi-car accident is inbound, cutting this conversation short. "Look, I've got to go. A car accident is coming in and they need me. I'll text you the info."

"Alright. Don't forget tomorrow. I'll meet you at your place at five."

"That's right. We're going to see Roland's band," I grumble at the thought of being around loud music. "Gotta go. See you then."

After disconnecting, I type out her information and hit send as I hurry down the hallway toward the incoming ambulance. This night was shit to start with... and it's getting shittier by the minute. The only saving grace is the young kid keeping my mind off the completely off-limits woman down the hall. This poor kid is lucky his injuries aren't severe, but I'm guessing his car wasn't so lucky. After taking a corner too fast, he wrapped his brand new mustang around a light pole. By some miracle, he only has a broken wrist and some minor lacerations. If I was a betting man, his pride is hurt more than anything else. Once I get him splinted, I head down to Poppy's room. I've barely made into her room when word comes in from the neurologist. He's tied up with surgery and has requested another scan in an hour to check the bleeding.

"Fuck." I swipe my hand down my face.

"I take it the consult didn't produce what you wanted?" Olsen slides in beside me, glancing at the screen in my hand.

Holding up the image, he hisses. "Shit. That's a nasty hematoma behind her eye. Makes me wonder how long she laid at the foot of the steps before they called someone." He shakes his head. "I'll go make a call to the PD while you handle them. That guy in there is a real piece of work. I almost want security to remove him."

"That bad?" I arch a brow at him.

He nods. "Yeah… that bad. Have fun with him. I'll let you know what they say."

Olsen disappears around the corner, undoubtably to run this case by our contact in investigations. Like me, he suspects its more than a simple slip. Knowing what Neuro wants in follow-up, I head back to speak with Poppy. Taking the results with me, I tap on the door and slip inside. Poppy looks like she's in a daze, a happy side effect of the pain medication she's on.

"Feeling alright, Ms. Jefferson?" I step to the edge of the bed and press along her shoulder, careful not to jostle her too much. With a head injury like hers, I know she's hurting.

"Mmmhum." She mumbles, her eyes staying locked on me as I move my hands along her arm.

I tip my head toward the nurse standing opposite me. "Get her prepped for another scan. Dr. Stein wants another run."

"CT? Didn't you already do one of those?" The man sitting in the corner stands abruptly at my mention of the word.

I glance over at him and scowl. "Yes. Another one. With her head injury and the first scan showing some swelling near the brain... the neurologist on call wants another one repeated."

"This is bullshit. It was just a clumsy little fall!"

"As you've said, but regardless of *how* it happened, a head injury is serious, especially if there's swelling—or, as the doctor is worried about, potentially bleeding around the brain. Neither is preferable, but one certainly has a far better prognosis. Either way, you're looking at a few more hours, at least before we know the extent of her injuries."

He purses his lips and growls. "I need to make a call."

The nurse and I watch as he storms out of the room, leaving us to prep her.

"What an asshole." Ashley, the nurse I reamed earlier, covers her mouth in shock. "Oh, my God. I'm so sorry Dr. Winston. That just slipped out."

"Don't worry about it, Ashley. He *is* an asshole." Her eyes widen for a moment, but she schools her expression quickly. "Now help me get her to radiology."

Together, we roll her down the hallway to the department. I'm thankful to see the x-ray tech is inside prepping. "Brian." I dip my chin. "Glad to see you here. Did neurology call you?"

"Yep. Said they wanted another look at this beautiful lady's brain."

I step into the room, refusing to leave her even for a moment. Seeing Poppy vulnerable makes my chest tighten. I know something more is going on with her—but until she tells me, there isn't much anyone can do.

I step beside the bed and smile beneath the face covering. "She's out?" I glance toward Brian, who stands at the head of her bed.

"Yep… she's a real character. Even in her drugged state earlier, she had some jokes."

I quirk a brow. "Is that so?"

Brian shakes his head as he chuckles. "She said—rather garbled… 'I want gauges hard. Turn it on, mmkay'."

Thankful for the mask hiding my face, I feel my lips quirk into understanding. This is the second time little Poppy has used my name, and I'm starting to think it's not a coincidence. My eyes flick to Brian, who is thankfully adjusting the machine. A quick scan of the room and I find it is just the three of us in the space. Brushing my gloved hand across her cheek, I lean down and whisper into her ear.

"Don't you worry, butterfly… I was turned on the moment you collided with my body in the park."

I move away quickly and turn to Brian. "Let's get her on the machine. I'm hoping it's nothing major."

"Me too. I'm hoping that first one was just inconclusive because she was squirming around a bit." He grimaces, looking down at her still form. "A woman like her deserves to be worshiped."

6

Gage

WALKING toward the back entrance of the venue where Roland is playing is like taking steps toward self-inflicted torture. And Drake hasn't missed my discomfort. Roland couriered backstage passes to his office yesterday, ensuring we didn't miss his show. As much as I hate this scene, it isn't new to us. We always enter through the employee doors when we come to a show. Usually, his security staff is here to greet us, but tonight it's the venue rent-a-cop guarding the door.

Security staff at the Mercedes Benz stadium are a bunch of young adults who get off on pretending to be cops. They love hassling any and everyone. Typically, we're dressed like the money we worked our asses off for, but tonight we went for a more casual look. Thinking of Drake in an Armani suit at a rock concert makes me laugh. I imagine our attire is why the pimple-face kid posted at the employee entrance thinks it's wise to give us a hard time. Not really in the mood for this, I'm about thirty seconds from exploding, but Roland steps out the door—and he looks even more pissed off. Glancing over at Drake, I realize he texted him to tell him.

"What's your name?" Roland stands within arm's reach of the young guard. His arms are tense across his chest as he speaks.

"Patrick, sir." The young kid's—yes, kid—voice wavers under Roland's pissed expression. Not only is the star of the show standing in front of him, but he's also chewing him out. I can only imagine what's going through his head.

"Do you realize you might single-handedly be the reason my show is delayed?"

"I was just doing my job." He blows out a breath and glances up at the sky. "I swear I wasn't trying to be a dick."

"Your job. Right. And did you notice their passes to be back here? Or were you more concerned with waving your tiny dick around pretending to be a cop? Because to me that's what this looks like." Roland motions us through the entrance. "You're done for the day, son. Run home to mommy and tell her how she fucked up raising you. Come on, bros. I don't have a lot of time to catch up thanks to this... shoulda been a cum stain."

I can't help but shake my head as we follow Roland up the stairs toward his dressing room. Roland is thirteen years younger than me—which usually means Roland's lingo is impossible for me to follow. I don't know what he's saying half the time. Not that he and Drake are any closer in age. He's a decade older than Roland.

"I've missed you, little brother." Drake tugs him into a hug as soon as we're inside the room. "How the hell have you been?"

"Good. The tour is almost done, so I'll be home in a few months." Roland plops down on the leather couch and rests his feet on the glass table. "I'm ready for a break, though."

"A break?" I share a confused glance with Drake at his admission. Roland has never once said he wants or needs a break.

"Is something wrong?" My brow quirks in question. "You've never taken a break."

Roland leans his head back and blows out an exaggerated breath. "I know. But I'm exhausted. I want to slow down and maybe write some new music. I've been moving non-stop for the last eighteen months and just need—"

"Rest?" Drake speaks. "I get it. You deserve to stop and enjoy the fruits of your hard work, Rol. No need to explain."

"Mr. Winston." A feminine voice has us turning toward the door. "They're asking for you backstage."

"Right." Roland stands and pops his neck. "Tell them I'll be right up, Isabella."

"Isabella?" I glance between Roland and the woman standing at the door.

"She's my public relations specialist. The label seemed to think I needed help with my image. They hired her a few months ago." A myriad of emotions scatters across his face but are gone almost as quickly.

"Your *image*? What the fuck does that mean?" I growl in irritation.

I get my brother has done some questionable things. But a public relations specialist? He's twenty-four years old and has more ambition than most kids his age. It's expected that he'd be in the tabloids for partying hard and being with a lot of women based on the lifestyle he leads.

"Apparently being filmed with various women is sending my fans the wrong message. Whatever. She just keeps the media at bay. No big deal."

"If you say so, little brother. But from the sound out there—" I point toward the hallway. "—your fans seem to love you just the same."

Roland cuts his eyes at us with a knowing look. "I gotta go. If she comes back in here, she'll bust my balls for sure. And despite the tabloids' wild opinions, that is *not* something I'd enjoy."

Roland hugs us before striding out into the corridor. The upside to having a famous musician for a brother. We get to watch from backstage. Drake and I hate the massive crowds that turn out for his music. And based on the roaring sounds coming from beyond the stage, the house is packed.

"Why the fuck would he need someone to help him with his image?" I grumble as I lean against the wall. "He hasn't been in the tabloids since last year—after that incident with the supermodel. I had no idea he had a public relations specialist. It's not like he's caught every other weekend with his dick out."

"Honestly, I'm not surprised they hired her. I told Roland eventually he would need to chill out. Maybe this will force him to focus on his music and stay out of the media's eye a bit." Drake shrugs his shoulders like this is no big deal. "Face it… the latest image is worse than the supermodel incident."

I know he's right. This latest stunt is pretty damning-still pisses me off they've given him a babysitter. My eyes follow

Roland as he bounces out onto the stage. His voice booms through the sound system, making the crowd go wild. "Welcome Atlanta." His voice echoes through the speakers. "Tonight is going to be fucking amazing. Are you ready?" he screams, causing everyone to erupt into shouts and cheers.

His words filter through the space, and I close my eyes and listen. My brother has some wicked talent, and part of me wonders if there is more to his music than just words on paper. While Roland had only been four when the shit went down with our parents, he closed himself off from relationships just like me and Drake. Well... *romantic* love. Listening to him sing each song so effortlessly makes my chest swell with pride. As he starts the next song, my phone vibrates in my pocket. Slipping it out enough to check the screen, I grimace.

"Fuck." I shoot Drake a look and step away enough to hear. "This is Dr. Winston."

"Winston." The familiar voice of Charles Hastings, head of Ortho, speaks. "I need you back at the ER. You've been requested by a patient's husband."

"Hastings, I'm not on call tonight. Call Peterson." I pinch the bridge of my nose, irritation filling my veins.

"No. He asked for you—the best orthopedic surgeon. Look, he's a big donor to the hospital and a judge. The board asked me to call you in. Do I need to say anything more?"

Grunting in disgust, I say, "Fine. I'll be there as soon as I can."

Shoving the phone in my pocket, I turn, not at all surprise to find Drake standing behind me.

"Everything alright?"

I run my fingers through my hair. "No. I have to go."

He glances back at Roland on stage, then back at me. "What? Now?"

"Apparently there's a judge in the waiting room demanding I come and see to his wife. The hospital board has requested my presence." The guilt of having to cut the visit short pisses me off and I blow out an exaggerated breath.

"Let's tell Roland we're leaving." Drake starts toward the edge of the stage.

I shake my head at him. "You can stay. I'll just grab an Uber."

Drake gives me a look that I know means there's no point in arguing with him. "Not a chance. If a judge is expecting you to drop your life and come in, I'm going with you. I want to make sure there isn't any unscrupulous intent behind this demand."

At that same moment, I hear Roland wrap up his song and tell the crowd he'll be back after a brief intermission. He tells the crowd that nature calls, and he needs to take care of business—which makes the stadium erupt into laughter.

"Whatdidya think?" Roland pops the lid to a water bottle and chugs its contents.

"Fantastic, as usual. Look." I grip his shoulder in my hand and squeeze. "I have to go. The hospital board called and demanded I come for a VIP patient."

"Really? Who is it? The King of Persia?" Roland chuckles.

"No, a local judge. And he's making a scene in the ER."

"You're going with him, right?" Roland turns toward Drake, the brilliant blue of his eyes filled with concern as he speaks.

"Of course. This request reeks of desperation and unscrupu-lousness." Drake nods, making Roland relax slightly.

"Good. Call me when you're done. Maybe you can meet up with me for a drink. I don't leave until tomorrow. Last stop is Austin, then home for a few months."

"Will do, little bro. Good show. I don't think your fans have lost their liking to you yet." Drake pats his back. We're inter-rupted by the PR girl as she steps beside him.

"Roland."

"Isabella." Roland's voice takes on a weird tone, making Drake shoot him a confused look. "These are my brothers, Gage and Drake." He motions to us.

"Um. Hi. I go by Izzy, though. Roland talks a lot about you." The glacier-level glare she gives him is not lost on me. "Can we talk for a moment?"

Roland stiffens, and I watch as the blood drains from his face. "*Now?*" His voice is laden with aggravation.

"Please?" I watch as she places her hand on his arm and he jerks away.

I glance between him and Isabella. "You good?"

"Yeah. Let me know how it goes." We watch as he turns and slowly follows Isabella toward his dressing room.

"What the hell was that about?" My head snaps to Drakes.

"I don't know, but I plan to find out. Let's go see what this judge wants so we can meet up with him later. Something is going on with him."

Security escorts us out, and we head to Drake's car. Frustration gets the better of me and I let out a massive breath as soon as I settle in the passenger seat.

"Are *you* good?" Drake tilts his head at me, his eyes narrowing on me in concern.

"Yeah. Just tired of the board jerking me around at the hospital."

"Why don't you start a private practice? It isn't like you don't have the money. Hell—I'd back you if you needed more."

"I wouldn't be able to help people in the same way, Drake." I've thought about it, more so lately. But helping people out of situations like my mom's is why I do this. I lean back on the headrest and close my eyes.

It takes no time to get to the hospital and before I know it, Drake's parked the car outside of the emergency room. We climb out and hurry inside through the ER entrance.

"Dr. Winston." One of the nurses runs toward us. "Thank God you came."

"Hey—you okay?" I reach out and stop her.

"Yes, but the—" Her words are interrupted as an older looking man approaches us from the patient area.

"Dr. Winston, it's about fucking time you got here."

"As I was saying—" The nurse shoots him an eat shit look and continues. "Judge Carmichael is here with his wife. She took a nasty spill down the stairs and injured her arm. He demanded that you be the one to assess her."

I notice Judge Carmichael give Drake a disgusted look, causing me to roll my own eyes. They know each other from interactions in court, and Drake has made it known he dislikes the man's methods. Judge Carmichael is the type of man that makes Drake's job infinitely harder. He sides with the husband in the case more often than not. From what Drake has told me, other attorneys have complained about his shitty skills on the bench.

"Fine. Take me to her. Drake." I face my brother. "Come back with me. You can wait at the nurses' station. After you, your Honor." Motioning for the judge to follow me through the double doors.

We head down a series of hallways before the nurse comes to a stop. "This is her room. I can show your brother where to wait. "

I nod as the Judge steps through the door. Drake is frozen to the floor outside the door, staring at the judge's wife—who visibly shudders when her husband moves beside the bed. Taking a deep breath, I shake off the concern and ease the door shut. But not before I see Drake and Mrs. Carmichael exchange a look.

Ignoring the oddity of their actions, I turn back to her. "Mrs. Carmichael. I'm Dr. Winston, the attending for orthopedics. I hear you took a bit of a fall."

7

Gage

"RIGHT. Of course. I forgot your pockets are deeper than mine. Calvin Winston was your father, after all."

Hearing Judge Carmichael spew the words like poison at Drake, I move a bit faster and interrupt. The last thing I need is for my brother to fly off the handle and punch the old bastard.

"Judge." I step beside him at the desk. "Your wife should be good to go in a couple of hours. I need to get another x-ray before putting her in a cast. I also want to get a CT to make sure there aren't any complications from hitting her head. She has a pretty nasty bump and a few bruises, but I think that's all. She's very lucky she didn't break her neck."

"Good—good." He pushes his shoulders back and stands taller. "Will Rhiannon be okay to attend the gala next weekend?"

Drake glances back into the room, and I narrow my eyes briefly on their silent exchange. Clearing my throat, to draw his attention away from her, I fill her husband in on her status. "She should be. That depends on the CT scan. If it shows any abnormalities, she'll need to miss it to rest. Doctor's orders."

A commotion at the front entrance draws my eyes toward an older man and woman practically running toward us.

"Where is she? Where's my Rhiannon?"

"Mr. Preston." Judge Carmichael turns to the man. "She's in there." He jerks his head toward her room.

"What the fuck happened?"

The older woman with him rushes into Rhiannon's room and wraps her arms around the patient. Clearly, they're her parents. I'm shocked when I realize who they are, and who *she* is. Lord knows they're always in the newspaper for something as owners of one of the largest shipping companies around. The woman, Mrs. Preston, has gray hair, and the years show on her face, but she's the older version of the woman lying in the bed.

"She tripped and took a spill down the stairs, Mr. Preston. This is Dr. Gage Winston. He's one of the top orthopedic surgeons in the nation. Dr. Winston, please let me introduce Mr. Preston—Rhiannon's father."

"Mr. Preston. I've heard a lot about you in the paper." I shift my stance and shake hands. "This is my brother, Drake Winston. We were together when I got the call, so he came along for the ride. Your daughter is going to be just fine, even though she broke the radius in her left arm. It won't require surgery, but will need to be immobilized. There is a possibility she'll need some physical therapy, but I won't know for certain for a couple of weeks."

"Thank God. I was scared out of my wits when my wife got the call from your groundskeeper."

Drake cuts his eyes toward the judge and speaks with such disdain even I flinch from his words. "*You* didn't call him?"

"I was more concerned with my wife," he spits out, his eyes filled with venom.

"And what do you do, Mr. Winston?" Her father turns to Drake. "You obviously know I own Preston Shipping, yet I'm not sure I know anything about you."

"I own Angel's Wings—an organization for people who can't or don't have the ability to grasp second chances when they've been living in hell." His eyes shift to Judge Carmichael as he speaks.

"Right." Her father stares Drake down, then finally looks over at me. "You're Calvin Winston's boys, aren't you?"

"Unfortunately." Not wanting to take a trip down memory lane, I interrupt. "If you'll excuse us. Drake?" I motion for Drake to follow me.

"Those two are the most pretentious pricks I've ever met in my life."

Raising one eyebrow, Drake's shoulder bumps into me as he follows me down the hall. "Where are you going?"

"My office. I need to take a minute to write up my notes. Maybe by the time I'm done, his wife's scans will be done." My office is on the third floor, plenty of distance to get myself calmed down.

"And you think she tripped down the stairs like they're claiming?"

"No." I can't stop the growl. "Her break is certainly consistent with falling down a flight of stairs. But the massive lump on the back of her head doesn't match her version of what happened."

"What's *her* version?" Drake sits opposite me as I plop down behind my desk.

"Both of them say she tripped going down the steps. Mrs. Carmichael says she put her arms out to brace her fall and went down them headfirst, breaking her arm as she landed on it. However, the lump on the back of her head says differently. Skulls don't just bruise without direct, blunt force trauma. And her break looks like she tried to grab the railing and twisted her arm as she fell. That, along with the cut to her temple with the bruises—bruises that look an awful lot like fingerprints, paired with the hematoma to her skull on the back that her husband has failed to mention, indicates she fell backward, not forward."

Drake says exactly what I was thinking. "*Fuck.*"

I nod and drop into my chair, pushing my fingers through my hair. "Yep. I'm pretty sure she was pushed. Or at a minimum, if she did fall, she was turned to block a blow to the face following several others that had already hit their mark."

Drake's foot taps nervously against the floor. "Did you ask her?"

"In a roundabout way. Her husband's a fucking judge—not to mention a huge financial donor to the hospital. I have to tread lightly about this."

"You think he's hurting her?" Drake glares at me, his voice dropping an octave.

As much as I hate to admit it, I'm pretty sure the pretty judge's wife is being harmed by him. I nod in agreement. "I do."

There's a slight tap at the door before it's pushed open. "Dr. Winston. That patient you asked us to notify you of—the one that came in a few days ago. She's back."

"I gotta go." I stand quickly, knocking my chair into the wall. "Call me later."

Drake grabs my arm and gives me a concerned look. "Do you need me to come down with you?"

I hesitate for a moment, but give him a quick shake of my head. "No—" and rush to the elevator. The entire ride down to the emergency room, my gut twists with unease. Poppy was released less than twenty-four hours ago. Her being here this soon can't be anything good. As soon as I step foot into the ER, I head straight for the nurse's station.

"What room is Poppy Jefferson in?"

The nurse glances up briefly, then hands me over an iPad. "12a."

Snatching the tablet from her grasp, I scan the screen. What I see has my blood boiling at volcanic levels. Seems Poppy tripped... again. I'm ready to go in her room and throat punch the motherfucker I think is responsible—the asshole who was with her last time.

Pushing inside her room, I jerk to a stop in surprise. Poppy is alone this time. "Where's your babysitter?"

Her head pops up and I regret my harsh tone immediately. Her eyes are black and blue, and the white of her pupil on the side where she injured it yesterday is bloodshot. The stitches from her fall are intact, but there is blood seeping out around the thread. Poppy quickly ducks her head, avoiding my gaze. I move without thought and gently ease her chin up to look at me.

"Don't tell me you fell, butterfly." I swipe at a tear that has escaped her eye.

A sob escapes her, and I can't stop myself from wrapping her in a gentle hug. She winces slightly, but I close my eyes in relief when I feel her body relax against mine. Her breaths rise and fall as I brush the locks of her hair. "You can't go back there, Poppy."

"I have nowhere to go," she whispers to me.

I want to scream, but I take a deep breath and sigh instead. "How about the police?"

She stiffens. "No. They won't stop him."

My eyes connect with Drake as he walks past the room, stopping to stare at me. He's never seen me hold a woman, so I know he wants to ask questions. Instead, he dips his chin and walks away. I'll have to answer him at some point, but right now, my only focus is on the woman crying in my arms.

"How are you here alone?" I ask, needing to know where the motherfucker is that did this to her.

She leans back and holds my gaze. "He was here, but something happened, and he had to go help my brother with another... *issue*. Don't worry. They'll be back."

There is no way in hell I can let this beautiful woman go. "You're not going home, Poppy."

Poppy pulls out of my arms and leans back against the bed. "And where exactly will I go? You don't get it, Gage. My brother—he's powerful. After our parents died, he decided he owned me. He gave me to his head of security."

"What do you mean, *gave*?"

She turns her head, so she's not looking at me. "Exactly as it sounds. Alessandro is my stepbrother. He wanted me for himself, but I told him I'd rather die than let that happen. He did the next best thing and betrothed me to Eduardo."

The names sound familiar. "Alessandro? Eduardo? Help me understand why you can't go to the police." I stand up from the bed and start toward the door, wanting to ensure it's closed.

"My stepbrother is Alessandro Hugo."

My head jerks toward her. "You're kidding, right?" Alessandro is known by many people for his criminal activity. He's not a man to trifle with, and I now know Poppy is lucky to be alive.

"No." Her voice is a whisper, but I can hear the pain in the one-word response.

All I can do is stare at this beautiful woman who has endured so much in her twenty-four years and the urge to pull her into my arms so I can shield her from the torment is over-whelming. She must sense the shift in my mood, because her gaze once again finds mine.

"I wish..." her words cut off and she glances down at her hands, which are twisting the sheet.

I move without hesitation and sit back down on the edge of the bed. "You wish what?"

I tilt her chin up gently. Her eyes, even the one that is red as fire, are wet with tears. She shakes her head, refusing to finish her words. But she doesn't need to. I already know what it is she wishes. And come hell or high water, I'm going to make it happen.

"I need to check you over." I stand and begin examining her. "Tell me if anything hurts to the point of being intolerable."

Poppy winces several times, but not to the point where I think she needs an x-ray—even though I should do exactly that. It would take too much time, and I don't plan on staying here much longer. As soon as I can confirm, to some degree, she isn't in danger medically—we're leaving.

"I think you've probably got another concussion. I'm going to clean up your sutures and then take care of things. Poppy." I cup her uninjured cheek. "Do you trust me?"

She holds my stare with her own and nods. "Yes."

That's all I need to hear. Standing, I go to the door and check the hallway. The nurse's station is clear of anyone, as is the hallway for the time being. Turning to face her, I say, "I want you to do something for me." She takes a deep breath and watches me push the door closed slightly. "I'm going to grab you a wheelchair. You're going to sit down, and I am going to push you down the hallway."

"Um... okay."

"Then you and I are going to take a little trip." I pull the door open and step out to retrieve a wheelchair that is pressed against the opposite wall. When I step back in, she's sitting on the edge of her bed with wide eyes. "Come on, butterfly, get in."

"What are you doing, Dr. Winston? I can't leave."

"You can and you will. I refuse to let you walk back into danger. Now get in this chair before your thug of a brother or his goon comes back. I promise to keep you safe until we get this worked out."

She hesitates, but slowly eases out of the bed. I hold my hand out to help her out of bed. "I don't understand why you're doing this. You could get in trouble or worse—"

I shake my head. "You're going to sign out against medical advisement. Here." She takes the tablet from my hand and scans the screen.

"I don't want to be the reason you lose your job. Because that's what will happen when my brother finds out what you've done." Her hand hovers above the glass screen.

"I don't care about my job. However, I care about *you*, butterfly. I don't know what that means, so don't ask me. All I know is I can't just turn a cheek and let you back into the lion's den. Let's go, Poppy. We're running out of time."

Her phone chirps on the bedside table and I watch as she glances down at it. Whatever she sees sparks something inside of her. "Fine." She tosses the phone onto the bed and climbs into the chair. "They're on their way back."

Without further ado, I turn her chair and hurry into the hallway. Laying the tablet on the nurse's station, I rush toward the elevators in the back hallway. Pressing the button for the third floor, I step inside, knowing that my decision will create a shitstorm—but when I see the anxiety Poppy is doing her best to hide from me, I know it's the right thing to do. She deserves freedom from the goons she calls family.

As soon as the doors slide open, I scan the floor and breathe a sigh of relief to find it empty. I've got to grab my keys so we can get the hell out of here. "Wait here." I park her outside my door and hurry inside to grab what I need. I take a second to snatch the key fob and get back into the hallway.

"Last chance to change your mind, butterfly. Stay here and wait for the devil... or trust I'm not a monster in disguise."

She regards me with scrutiny, bloodshot eye and all. The light that I would expect to see in such a young, vibrant girl is nowhere to be seen. With a slight tip of her head and a softly whispered 'yes', I push her toward the bank of elevators that will take us to the employee parking garage.

I've only ever been scared once in my life. It was when I wrestled my father for the gun pointing at me, and when I pulled the trigger to end his life after he took my mother's.

But right now... as I push Poppy toward my waiting SUV, I'm terrified. Not because of who her brother is or that I might lose my job. *No.* I'm scared shitless because of the emotions this woman invokes in me.

Emotions, I swore I'd never let myself feel again.

8

Poppy

I'M silent as Gage helps me into the passenger seat. I watch as he rounds the front and climbs in. The sun is beginning to set, painting the sky in pink and purple hues. The throbbing pain pulsing in my head has simmered some, and I don't feel the need to squint at the glow still burning what's left of the daylight.

Gage pulls out of the parking garage, still not saying anything as he turns onto the busy downtown streets. I listen as he calls the hospital, explaining he had a family emergency and had to leave. He tells whoever is on the other end he isn't sure when he will be back and that he'll contact HR to work it out. I know I should ask questions, but I'm still in shock. This man is risking *everything* to help me, and I can't for the life of me fathom why. It isn't until we pull down a long driveway that I finally muster up the courage to speak.

"Where are we?" The property is nearly as large as the one my brother owns, but this one doesn't feel like I'm entering a prison.

"My house." Gage parks the vehicle and cuts the engine. "This is a temporary stop until I can work something out." He climbs out and slams the door. Once again, he's at my side, helping me out. Gage brushes his knuckles down the side of my face. "You're safe here, butterfly. I promise."

Nodding my head, I follow him up a set of steps and step into the house behind him. The inside is not what I expect. It's got a rustic vibe that screams bachelor—but not in a frat boy kind of way. I'm not sure what I'm supposed to do, and Gage must sense my apprehension.

"Come on. Let's go sit down and talk. I think there's more I need to know, and then we need to come up with a game plan."

Following him through the hallway, I notice right away there are only photos of him and who I assume must be his brothers.

"Roland Winston is your brother?" I shake my head at the realization that this man is related to the lead singer of the Savage Realm, but Gage only shrugs at my question. He's probably used to women asking about him, but I could not care less—he's not the one who has me all twisted up on the inside.

Aside from Roland's picture, only one other photo stands out among the others. It's the only one with a woman. "That your mother?" I point to the image of her smiling between the three boys.

"No." His gruff tone makes me stiffen. Assuming it's not a subject he wants to talk about, I push past him and plop into a chair. "Shit... I'm sorry Poppy. It's just—" he sighs and pulls out the chair beside me. He pulls my hands into his and leans forward. "My life isn't pretty. There are things about me I want to tell you, but first, we need to figure out where to go from here. The rest can wait."

"It's fine. Really. You're not the only one whose life isn't sunshine and rainbows." I pull my hands free and fold them into my lap. "Maybe I should just go back."

He leans back in the chair and narrows his eyes on me. "Is that what you want? To go back and let him beat you some more?"

I flinch at how his words pierce my very soul. They're hurtful, but true. I try to mask my emotions, but Gage seems to know how I feel even when I try to hide it.

"Poppy. I didn't mean it to be ugly. But I want to help you—will you let me do that?"

"I…" My voice cracks and I can't stop the tears. Gage lifts me from my chair and places me in his lap. He cradles me against his chest, his hand smoothing my hair down my back.

"Butterfly…" The nickname he's given me rolls off his tongue as a whisper, yet it still has the same effect on me—and I don't know what to do with this tangled web of emotions. "You deserve to spread your wings and fly—not be trapped in the spider's web."

"What do you get out of helping me, Gage? I'm nobody to you." I bury my face in his scrub top and inhale his scent. I can't look at him because, for one, I look like the bride of Frankenstein. And two, I don't want him to see the fucked-up hope hiding in my eyes.

His silence feels like a gut punch, and I attempt to crawl from his hold, but his arms tighten around me. "Stay." Gage's single-word command halts my movement. "I don't ever want to hear you reduce yourself to nothing again. And as far as helping you, I'm not sure I can answer that right now—because I'm not sure the reason I tell myself holds any truth. I know this—" he takes a breath. "I wish someone had been there for my mother. Maybe then my brothers and I wouldn't have been forced to grow up as fast."

Gage eases me off his lap, placing me in the chair before standing. "I need to make a phone call. Let me show you where the shower is. I want you to wash all essence of that motherfucker from your skin, Poppy." He grabs a trash bag. "Put your clothes in this. I'll bring you something to change into that isn't tainted with *him*."

Confused is an understatement as to how I'm feeling right now. Wordlessly, I follow him up the stairs, bypassing several rooms, and step into a massive room behind him. "This is my room. Use my bathroom through there." He points, smiling as I stand frozen to the spot. "Go ahead... I'll bring you something to wear in a bit." Gage waits for me to walk around him.

Taking that as my cue, I walk into the bathroom—one that makes mine at home look like child's play. It's damn near as large as his bedroom. The clawfoot tub sits off to one side, while a custom shower fills the other. Two doors are on the opposite wall, which I guess lead to a closet and toilet. I stare at the shower and decide I want to soak in the tub. Stepping in front of the vanity, I gasp. My face is several shades of blue, and the stitches from the first time Gage saw me in the ER are caked with dried blood. My raccoon eyes give me the appearance of someone who either just had one hell of a bender or lost a boxing match—either isn't a great reason.

Turning toward the porcelain soaker, I cut on the water and strip off my clothes. Sinking into the steaming water, I drape my arms over the edges and sink into the heat. My life is a complete fucking train wreck and I'm not sure being in a house with a man I want more than I've ever wanted someone before is wise. He's already marked himself for death by helping me. Giving Gage the one thing I refuse to give Eduardo would be the nail in the coffin—probably for both of us.

The squeak of the door has me opening my eyes. Gage steps through, carrying a towel and some clothes. "Poppy, I'm going to—"

His words die on his lips when his eyes connect with mine. He lurches to a standstill, his gaze frozen on the tips of my nipples that peek out from beneath the bath water. "I thought you were in the shower."

I glance toward the amber brown glass and shake my head. "I didn't think you'd mind if I used the tub." I use my toes to flick the faucet off, his gaze trailing the length of my leg sticking out from the surface.

"I... ah—I." He palms the back of his neck and swallows. "I uh... brought you these." He holds up the stack in his hands. "I should go." Gage sets the items down and turns his back to me. He grips the edge of the door, his shoulders raised as he blows out a breath, but doesn't move.

"Gage?" I can see the struggle he's having based on the stiffness of his body.

"I shouldn't have come in here," he whispers. "Tell me to go, Poppy. Tell me to walk out of this bathroom right now."

I don't speak, I can't. The truth is, I don't *want* him to leave.

I finally find my voice. "And if I don't?"

Gage growls, his fingers digging into the wooden frame as he seems to have a conversation with himself. "Those are dangerous words, butterfly."

He steps out and slams the door, the sound causing me to jump. I want to believe my current state isn't the reason he stormed out, but I can't help thinking my being damaged made him run. The water has lost its luster and I toe the stopper out, watching as the water slowly descends into the drain. Easing out of the tub, I stand and stare at myself in the mirror. After the first beating from Alessandro, I learned that defending myself made it worse. Then Eduardo joined the fun, striking out at me in fits of rage when I wouldn't give in and let him take my virginity. I shudder, thinking about the things he made me do, wishing like hell he hadn't gotten those 'firsts' either.

Grabbing the towel Gage left for me, I dry myself off and grab the stack of clothes he left behind. He left me a pair of sweats and a t-shirt. The cotton pants are huge, so I forgo them and only slip on the t-shirt. It's practically a dress, hitting me at the top of my knees, so it covers me plenty. I'm thankful for its length, since I am without underwear at the moment. Toweling my hair, which is only wet at the ends, I give up and turn to leave. Pausing at the door, I take a deep breath and ready myself to face him.

I should be scared of my stepbrother and his henchmen coming for me... but the only thing I'm frightened of is waiting for me on the other side of the door. And this fear isn't terror.

It's a fear of him not wanting me the way I want him.

9

Gage

IT TOOK every ounce of willpower to turn around and walk away from her naked body. I knew she was beautiful, but fuck—the reality is nothing like I imagined. My cock is so fucking hard, I'm pretty sure it's about to rip open my scrub bottoms. I move to the bed and climb in, resting my head against the wall as I try to take several breaths to calm my raging need.

If she had been any other woman, I would have dragged her out of the tub and fucked her against the counter. But she's different from the women I usually have sex with. For one, she's not tied up. That confuses me even more. Usually, I need the binds around their delicate flesh to get off—it's just the way I like things. It gives me a sense of control.

But my cock didn't seem to get the memo. I untie the string holding my pants up and loosen the waist, needing to relieve some of the pressure my hard-on is creating inside the cotton. Flicking my eyes toward the door of the bathroom, I wonder if she's still soaking beneath the translucent water. Of course, that does nothing to help my dick, and I absentmindedly reach beneath the elastic band of my boxers to touch myself.

Hissing at the sensation of my fingers wrapped around my shaft, I close my eyes and stroke myself. Her being in the bathroom no longer matters. I must do *something* or I'm going to go back in there and take what I want. My hand works my cock as I conjure the image of her nipple caught between my teeth. "Fuck." I grunt, my balls tingling as I speed up. Using my free hand, I shove the material out of the way of the impending explosion I feel building in my spine.

My breathing speeds up as the prickling sensation burns its way down my back, zipping through my rigid member as the orgasm barrels through me. My eyes clench shut, and I arch my back, crying out Poppy's name, as the cum spurts from the tip, coating the work shirt I still have on.

I stroke it one more time before letting go and sliding my feet off the bed. Using the already ruined top, I wipe my hands clean and then pull it over my head. I hear the sound of the tub draining and my body seizes with the realization of what I just did. Something about this woman has my common sense completely muddled.

I grab my cell phone off the dresser and leave the bedroom to call Archer. Padding down the stairs, I plop myself on the couch and groan. I swore I'd never let a woman control me, but the more I am around her, I realize—Poppy has the power to not only control me, but dominate me in ways I'm not prepared for.

Searching for Archer Town's number, I press the button and turn it on speaker. He's the only one I can think of to get us somewhere safe until I come up with a plan.

"Gage? To what do I owe this late-night call?" Archer's tone is sarcastic as he answers. He's my brother's head of security and damn good at his job.

"Archer, I've got a situation."

He sighs into the line. "Let me guess… it has to do with a *Poppy Jefferson?*"

"Yes." I shove my fingers through my hair and grunt. "How'd you know?"

"Drake asked me to dig into her."

I want to tell him that this isn't as bad as it looks, but I can't lie. "It's not what he thinks. She's in trouble and I couldn't let her go back to her stepbrother. He's been hurting her, Archer."

"And we have something in place for cases just like this. Tell her to come to Angel's Wings. We'll handle it."

"She's here." I lean back against the chair. "And that's where she'll stay. But we need a safe house. As soon as her brother realizes she left the ER with *me*, he'll come for us."

"Right… because her brother is one of the foremost known gang leaders in the Atlanta area? Jesus Christ, Gage. What are you thinking?"

"That I want to keep her safe—no, I *need* to keep her safe. Please, Archer."

He is silent on the other end, making me nervous. If he isn't willing to move us, we're going to be in a world of hurt. "I'm already climbing into my car, Gage. Be ready to move—you've just painted an enormous target on yourself." He pauses. "You do realize this won't end well, right? What about your job?"

"I'll take a leave of absence, but Archer..." I glance up at the sound of footsteps.

Poppy has padded her way into the room and stops in front of me. Her expression is riddled with confusion when she hears my words to Archer. "I'd quit if it meant protecting what's mine."

Archer says something, but I can't hear a word he's saying because my eyes are riveted to the woman standing before me. "See you soon." I toss the phone to the table beside me, never taking my eyes off Poppy.

"What's the matter, butterfly?"

I watch as her chest rises with each intake of air, and I don't miss how her fingers twist the fabric of her shirt. "Where will we go? Once Eduardo realizes I'm gone, he'll come for us— he'll kill us both, Gage."

"I'm working on it, Poppy. For now, we wait on Archer." I shift my legs and stand, putting some distance between us. "I couldn't save my mother... but I won't fail you."

Her sharp intake of breath causes me to turn and look at her. The expression she wears is like a knife to the heart and my shoulders droop. "Am I just a project to you? Is that what this is?"

Pinching the bridge of my nose, I sigh. "No. You're not a project, you're—" a knock at the door interrupts our conversation. Poppy's eyes dim with understanding that this conversation is over for now. Moving to the door, I yank it open to find Archer standing on the other side.

"That was quick," I growl, motioning him inside.

He glances at Poppy's state of dress and gives me a look. "Well, you didn't exactly leave work without drawing attention. We need to leave... *now*."

After a tense stare down, Archer loads us into his car. His raised eyebrow and constant glare in the rearview mirror tell me he knows something more is happening between Poppy and I. "Care to tell me where we're going?"

I smirk at him from the backseat, my fingers twirling Poppy's hair as she sleeps against my shoulder. My need to be close to her is just as confusing to me as it is to Archer, so if he asked me right now what that was—I wouldn't have an answer for him.

"A safe house like you asked. You'll have one guard with you at all times until we figure out what to do." He shakes his head. "I knew the day you or your brothers fell for a woman, it was going to be messy... but fuck, brother... you had to go and pick the hardest damn dame out there, didn't you?"

I glance down at her sleeping face and frown. "I haven't fallen for her. She just needs someone to protect her."

"Okay. You keep telling yourself that, Gage." He reaches over and opens the glove box. I watch in horror as he removes a Glock and shuts it back. "In the meantime." He stretches his arm over the seat and holds it out to me. "Take this. You might very well need it."

I stare at the weapon, bile rising in my throat. "No." I flick my eyes to his. "You know I don't touch those things."

Archer sighs, his arm dropping so he can rest the gun on the back of the seat. "I know, Gage. But this is a situation where you're going to need something to protect yourself. Take the gun."

Ever since the night I shot my father, I've steered clear of weapons. It was something I promised myself I would never touch again. Instead, I became a doctor—it's my job to save lives, not take them.

"I can't." I lean back, turning my head to look out the window. "I'm sorry, that's a hard no for me."

Archer slides the Glock over the seat and lays it in the seat next to him. "Fine. But I'm going to leave it at the safe house. Touch it, don't touch it—that's up to you. But Gage—" he looks at me through the mirror. "With the path you've chosen… you might not have a choice."

Glancing down at Poppy, I swallow the bitterness rising in my throat. Even though I'll do anything to protect her… I don't know if I can do *that*. After what feels like an eternity, Archer pulls down a residential street and stops in front of a small house.

"This is it." He kills the engine and climbs out, leaving me alone with Poppy.

Brushing my hand across her shoulder, I lean down and press my lips to her ear. "Butterfly… we're here."

She grumbles something but doesn't seem to wake. I slide out from under her and push open my door. Leaning down into the car, I slide her out and scoop her into my arms. Her eyes flutter, but the exhaustion of the last twenty-four hours has wiped her out completely. Archer raises an eyebrow at me but says nothing. I know he's confused by my behavior— he knows what kind of man I am. Seeing me carry a woman who's in my t-shirt, has him stumped.

Not to mention I'm risking both my career *and* life for her.

"Bedrooms down the hall."

I nod, carrying Poppy to the bedroom in the back. Gently laying her down, I tug the blanket folded at the end of the bed over her bare legs. Glancing at her one more time, I back out of the room and leave the door cracked. Archer and I need to figure out where to go from here. By now, there's no doubt her brother knows I have her.

"What's the plan?" Archer is watching me with narrowed eyes as I step into the living room.

He folds his arms across his chest and blows out a frustrated sigh. "Part of me wants to choke the shit out of you, Gage. But I see how you looked at her in the car—I never thought I'd see the day when the mighty Gage Winston lost his soul to a woman." He motions to the couch. "You picked one hell of a lady to tangle yourself with."

"I didn't plan for this, Archer. I'm just as stunned as you are, but there is something telling me I have to help her. My brothers and I all live by a code… we didn't exactly have the best example growing up, and I never wanted to let that darkness taint someone. Hell—maybe this is some kind of way to atone for my past."

"Atone for your past? Because of your father? Gage, neither you nor your brothers are anything like your father. And you don't owe a damn thing to anyone for the sins of that man."

"I'm not a good man, regardless of whose blood runs through my veins. I've made life choices that she wouldn't under-stand." My brow arches as I frown at him.

He actually laughs. "And who says *she's* a good woman? You don't know a thing about her. What if she's some kind of sexual deviant seeking to trap *you*?"

I scrub my hand down my face. "She's not."

Archer narrows his eyes at me. "How do you know that?"

Growling, I throw both hands in the air. "I *don't*. But I feel... *different* around her. The attraction to her isn't like that. Sex has always been driven by my need to control the environment—the thought of marking her skin with rope makes me uneasy."

His gaze is on me as I talk. Archer is aware of the things my brothers and I like when it comes to sex. He's had to clean up some lingering issues surrounding some of our hook-ups—more so on Roland's end. Which is why I only use the club now. Thoughts of tainting Poppy's light with my sordid past makes my stomach coil with disgust.

"And *that's* the look I saw earlier." Archer points to my face. "This is more than simply helping someone in need, Gage. You need to accept that because you're going to need every ounce of emotion to fight what's coming. Alessandro Hugo's not a man who simply walks away. You need to call Drake and get legal protection in place. Otherwise..."

He doesn't have to say it, because I am knowledgeable enough about the criminal dealings of Poppy's stepbrother to know what kind of shit storm I've created by taking her away from him. "I know. That's why I called you. It won't take him long to put two and two together, and it's easy to find out where I live. Hell, he could pay someone at the hospital for that information. Everyone can be bought."

"For now, stay here." Archer stands and moves toward the door. "One of my guys will be here with you. He's outside right now, walking the perimeter. This might be a residential area, but don't put it past Hugo or his thugs to hunt you down. Her boyfriend is nearly as ruthless as her stepbrother.

They're going to assume there is something more between you… and your dick will be on his chopping block."

I wince at the thought of my cock being hacked from my body. "I'd like to keep those parts intact."

"If you suspect anything is amiss, you tell Danny. I'll text you his number. Gage, this is not a fucking joke, okay? Hugo will come for you sooner rather than later. And this isn't something your money can get you out of."

I blow out a deep breath, watching as Archer leaves the house. I know the next call I make will not be as easy. Needing to check on Poppy, I slowly make my way upstairs. There is no explanation for my actions other than I want what I shouldn't. As I push open the door, my phone vibrates inside my pocket. Drake's face fills the screen. Taking a deep breath, I press the speaker button.

"Drake."

"Gage, what in the *fuck* are you doing?" His voice is filled with the anger I expected.

"I know you're pissed—"

He cuts me off. "Pissed?" He laughs, the sound manic. "Pissed doesn't even cover it. Do you realize who that woman is? Why *her*, Gage? You've helped hundreds of women over the years. What makes this one different?"

"I can't explain it, Drake. But I need to make sure she's safe. I'll be taking a leave of absence from the hospital. I'll need you to cover for me at the Gala."

"Do you hear yourself? *Fuck*." I hear him take several breaths. "Her brother is a sick motherfucker, Gage. If he doesn't come for you, her boyfriend will. Are you ready to deal with that? Do you have a death wish?"

"I need you to file the appropriate paperwork to protect her. She needs out of that life and out from under her brother's thumb. He doesn't care about her well-being or the fact his right-hand man is beating her. And I'm going to help her—whatever that means. One day you'll understand."

"Understand what?"

"Poppy has been coming into my ER for months, Drake. I couldn't stand by and watch him kill her. She's too scared to go to the police. This was the only way."

"Then bring her here. Let me set her up with Angel's Wings. My people can help her start over."

"No. I'm helping her. Look." I glance up to see Poppy's eyes on me. "She's waking up. I need to make sure she's good. I'll call you later. And Drake?" I lower my voice as I step toward the bed where she lays. "Please do this for me."

"Fine. I'll call you when I have everything done. Be careful, brother. I feel you're getting in deeper than you realize, and it'll be too late to undo it." Drake sighs, and I know he's mad at me, but also afraid. He knows what Hugo and his men are capable of.

"It's already too late. I'll talk to you soon."

I drop the phone onto the dresser's surface and pause. "Are you feeling okay?" I glance over at Poppy, who is watching me with apprehension.

"I can leave, Gage. I don't want to make this difficult for you or your family. Whoever you were talking to is right... my brother will stop at nothing to drag me home."

My feet carry me to the bed as though they have a mind of their own and I stare down at her.

My heart stutters at the hopelessness I see reflecting in her eyes and it sends me back to the moment I watched my mother take her last breath. A moment I swore I'd never witness again. But looking at this woman's face, I have to consider Archer might be right. Maybe this is more than just needing to protect her, and that is something I refuse to admit right now.

"Let's not worry about that." I motion for her to slide over. "Right now, I need some sleep and so do you. Tomorrow we'll talk about everything, okay?" Poppy nods, her eyes wide as she watches me slip beneath the covers. "I hope this is okay. I don't want to leave you unattended."

"It's fine."

I close my eyes, forcing away the desire to hold her against me, and let sleep claim me. This woman is unraveling my tightly knit boundaries and I don't know if I can stop it—or if I want to.

10

Gage

I BOLT UP IN BED, knowing immediately something's wrong. Glancing at Poppy, I sigh in relief that she's still conked out. Whatever's torn me from my sleep has nothing to do with her being beside me. I slip out from beneath her arm, careful not to disturb her and make my way out into the hallway. I find Danny in the living room, his gun drawn.

"What is it?" I glance toward the front window, seeing nothing but darkness.

He presses his fingers to his lips, urging me to be quiet, and ticks his head in the direction of the front door. "Where's Poppy?"

"Asleep." I glance back at him. "Should I go wake her?"

He nods, inching his way closer. "Yes. You two need to be ready to leave if it comes down to your safety."

Spinning on my heel, I race up the stairs and step into the room. I grab my jeans, tugging them in place as I move toward the bed. "Butterfly." I caress her shoulder, dragging my hand down her arm and lace our fingers. Tugging her knuckles to my lips, I press a gentle kiss across her delicate skin, ignoring the way my body responds to the taste of her flesh.

She mumbles something as her eyes slowly open. It takes her a second to get her bearings. "Gage?" She shifts to sit up. "What's going on?"

"Not sure. Danny is downstairs checking it out, but it looks like someone might have tried to break in."

She gasps, her body going rigid. "Alessandro." Her voice cracks and I see the terror in her eyes, despite the darkness she's bathed in.

Pressing my other palm to her cheek, I brush my thumb over her lip. "It may be nothing. But Danny said we need to be ready to move."

We're about to walk into the hallway when Danny knocks on the door. "Can I come in?"

I pull the door open, allowing him to step inside. "Turn on the light, butterfly."

Poppy flicks on the bedside lamp as I take a seat beside her. "Well? Is it my stepbrother? Has he found us?" She twists her fingers in her lap, the anxiety rolling off her in tidal waves.

"No. It was a false alarm. Stray cat was looking for somewhere to go. I've cleared the perimeter and ensured that no one is here. I'm sorry to have alarmed you. You two can go back to bed."

This situation is spiraling every hour that passes, and I know Poppy is starting to lose hope. I can see it in the tension her body holds, and it makes me want to scream. She leans against me and sighs. My fingers thread through her hair and I pull her against me tighter. There's nothing more I want than to stop this train's collision course, but it feels like an impossible situation. I wonder if going through Drake's organization would've been smarter, but it's too late now.

"I'm sorry, Gage. I really didn't mean for you to get involved like this."

"You'd rather be dead or Eduardo taking what doesn't belong to him?" I growl, giving Danny a simple nod as he silently exits the room.

She shakes her head against me. "No. I just—" She turns away from me, giving me her back. "Is it too much to ask for a normal life? I'm almost twenty-five and I have nothing to show for myself other than some bruises and scars. What does that say about me?"

"That you've lived through hell. Besides." I tighten my arm around her. "You have me... and that may not be a big deal to you, but I promise I won't leave you on your own. When this is all said and done, butterfly, you'll want for nothing."

"How can you say that?" She holds my gaze. "You're probably going to be jobless because of me."

"It doesn't matter." I press my lips to her forehead. "I'm a billionaire. It's not like I need to work, anyway."

Rolling away from her, I flop to my back and stare at the ceiling. Maybe Drake was right. Maybe it's time I open my own practice for Angels Wings. Poppy rolls to face me and props herself up with her arm.

She's staring at me with a mixture of disbelief and aggravation. "You can't just drop a bomb like that and act like it isn't something major."

I turn my head in her direction. "What bomb?"

She blows out a frustrated breath. "The one about being a billionaire."

"It's nothing... and I like that you're lying beside me, acting shocked." I smirk, rolling my eyes at her.

She narrows her eyes at me. "I *am* shocked. I didn't know who you were in the park... and apparently I still don't." Poppy slides from the bed and I watch as she pads to the bathroom and slams the door closed. The framed store-bought image hanging on the wall rattles with the force of the door before crashing to the floor.

I scrub my palm over my face, disgusted with my stupid assumption. "*Fuck*." Every other woman tries to garner my attention because of what I have, not who I am.

I know she's not like *them,* and implying she is—was an asshole thing to do. I climb from the bed and walk to the door. Pausing, I press my hand to the door and take a deep breath—I don't want her to see me as the coldhearted prick everyone else does. The need for her to see me for *me* is over-whelming. Turning the knob, I push open the door slowly. Poppy is sitting on the lid of the toilet, her eyes red and wet with tears. Knowing I caused her to be upset pierces me straight to the core and my heart clenches beneath my sternum.

"I'm sorry, butterfly. I shouldn't have implied you knew about my money. I kinda assumed. I'm used to women climbing into bed with me because of my fat wallet. But that's not you, and I know it. It's one of the reasons I want to help you."

Poppy looks down at her feet. "I couldn't care less if you lived in a box. You're not like my stepbrother or Eduardo. You don't flash your money around or use it to intimidate people."

"Look at me, butterfly." I take a step toward her, willing her to look up.

She shakes her head no. "I should just go."

I'm on her in a flash. "No." I cup her chin, lifting her face so I can peer into her jade eyes. "If you go, you're as good as dead, Poppy. Please don't make me watch someone else I care about die at the hands of a monster."

She gasps, her eyes widening. "What?"

"I need you to listen to me and really hear what I'm about to tell you." I take a breath. "When I watched my father kill my mother and then the life drain from his eyes when I pulled the trigger, I swore I would never let someone get under my skin like my mom had let my dad. He had so much power over her, making her lose herself. I've always believed caring about a woman was a prison, locking a person into a cage and giving away all the power over them." I swallow the nerves, letting go of her face and turn away from her. "But I was wrong. Caring for another isn't a prison."

"I don't understand, Gage." I don't dare turn around to look at her.

I wrap my fingers around the doorknob. "You have the power to destroy me completely, Poppy." The admission comes out in a whisper, my eyes closing at the scary realization that Archer is right, and I leave the bathroom.

Poppy rushes out behind me and wraps her arms around my middle. "Gage."

I spin her around and crash my lips to hers. My fingers thread through her hair, pulling her as close to me as I can get. When I break free, her eyes are glazed over with a hazy look of lust. "There are things you need to know about me, Poppy. Things that I crave that keeps the tainted blood coursing through my veins at bay. Things that might terrify you and I don't want that to destroy your light. But—" I close my eyes, needing to block her from seeing the fear in my eyes.

Her palm presses against my cheek. "Gage… I've lived in hell since my mom died. Nothing, and I mean *nothing,* could compare."

Sitting on the edge of the bed, I press my hands to my face. Everything I've done to guard myself from the feeling burning in my chest hits me like an avalanche, burying me under the guilt of my past decisions. It's not as though I'm a monster—not completely. Everything I've done has been consensual, but this woman doesn't deserve the tainted past I carry around. Suddenly, my promiscuity feels dirty.

Poppy climbs on the bed, her hands winding around my middle as her lips press against my back. "Tell me." She whispers against my flesh, the heat of her breath filling me with emotions I've held at bay for nearly twenty years. Not even when I was handcuffed and drug from my childhood home did I break.

I couldn't.

Drake and Roland needed me to be strong for them. Not even after I left for college and poured myself into my studies did I shed a tear. But as she peppers my back with tender kisses, I crack. My soul ripping open like a fissure in the ground, threatening to swallow me whole.

"Gage." Poppy slides around me and drops to the floor in front of me. Her hands wrap around my neck as she presses her forehead against mine. "Let me help you carry the pain, like you help me. *Tell me.*"

"I *killed* my father, Poppy. *Me*, his own son." The tears fall like rain, wetting the sheet loosely draped across my jean-clad legs. "And I couldn't save her—the woman who gave me life."

"It's not your fault. You were a child, Gage—a *child*." She wipes away the tears with her thumb. "This is why you became a doctor, isn't it?" I nod, words still missing from my vocabulary. "You couldn't have stopped what happened. What if it had been Drake? Or your younger brother? Your father got off easy, Gage. I hope he's in the pits of hell burning for what he did to you. But stop blaming yourself for the actions of an adult. It's *his* fault. Not yours. And not your brothers', either."

"He made me who I am, Poppy." I finally speak. "I need to be in control, or I might turn into him."

She cups my face with both hands. "Not possible. Control doesn't make you evil unless you're using it to hurt someone. Will you hurt me, Gage?"

11

Poppy

His eyes are glazed with unshed tears as he holds my gaze and answers without hesitation. "Never."

I can't believe this man has been holding on to the guilt for something he had no choice but to do. It's something he should've never faced as a child. And though I've lived in my own torment for the last few years, it's nothing compared to the burden this beautiful man has carried. His hurt goes deep and all I want to do it wipe it from existence. I *ache* for him. Like a bolt of lightning, I realize I've fallen in love with him. He might not feel the same for me, but I intend to help him carry the burden, anyway.

"Then you're worrying for nothing." I lean my forehead against his again and sigh. "This connection I feel with you is overwhelming, Gage. But I know in my heart of hearts it's meant to be. I can't explain it—but I think you walking away from me would hurt more than a thousand blows from Eduardo or Alessandro. Don't run… *please.*"

His breaths are ragged as he inhales. I know he's battling the darkness he thinks he carries inside—but they're only ghosts of his past. "I want you to share everything with me, Gage. Nothing you can do or say will make me walk away willingly."

A soft knock at the door startles me. Gage doesn't speak. He simply slides out from my grasp and stands. I watch as he shuffles toward the door, pulling it open enough to press his head through the crack. The muscles of his shoulders flex with tension as he speaks in hushed tones, to who I assume is Danny on the other side of the door. When he opens the door a little wider, I watch as a hand reaches through the opening and drops a bag to the floor.

Gage pushes the door closed and turns to face me. "Archer brought some essentials. Clothes, toiletries—stuff. We should shower and eat something."

He lifts the bag from the floor and sets it on the dresser. I watch as his body stiffens momentarily but seems to brush whatever it was it off quickly. He tugs out the contents, setting them on the surface. Gage grabs the bag and shoves it inside one of the drawers. "I'll be in the shower."

The sudden coolness in his tone has me worried, so I clamber from the bed and wander over to the dresser. I rifle through the things out in the open, finding nothing that would explain why he left me to shower alone. Yanking the drawer open, I pull out the bag and peer inside. At the bottom of the duffle bag is a gun—knowing what he's been through, I realize this must have been what triggered him. But what's coiled beside the gun piques my interest. Reaching inside, I brush my fingers across the smooth twine and jerk my hand back, startled. The fact he has a gun and rope should freak me out, but growing up around Alessandro and Eduardo, it doesn't.

I refuse to let him shut me out now. Not when we've shared so much in such a short amount of time. Grabbing the toiletries, I stalk toward the bathroom. Gage has his hands pressed against the tile wall with his head bowed beneath the spray of the water. He seems to be lost in thought and doesn't act like he hears me come in. Laying the items down on the counter, I take a deep breath and pull open the glass door, making my presence known immediately.

Gage doesn't turn to look at me. "I need to be alone, Poppy."

"No." I glare at him, ignoring the fact he is completely naked. "I don't know what happened out there, but you don't get to shut me out, Gage. Not after what we shared just now."

He straightens, dropping his hands from the wall, and takes a deep breath. "You don't get to make demands of me because I'm helping you out. " He spins around me and steps out, leaving me to stare at the space where he once stood.

It feels as though a knife has been pressed between my breasts, penetrating my beating heart, and I struggle to breathe. The sound of the bathroom door slamming sends me to my knees, the pain of impact barely noticeable over the one in my chest. His words burn my mind as I replay them over and over in my head. I thought he cared for me... at least, he said he did. I practically *said* the words to him—now I'm glad I didn't.

I tilt my head into the falling water as the sob rips free. Did I spend the last few years guarding my heart from the devil... only to give it a monster? Curling up on the cool floor of the shower, I draw my knees to my chest and give in to the hurt of his words. Lost to the pain, I don't register the shirt I wear clinging to my skin as it soaks beneath the spray of the water. How could I have been so stupid?

Lost in the darkness, I barely register the spicket cutting off. My body shakes as warm arms slide beneath my sodden frame. They carry me to the counter and set me down.

Fingers brush away the wet locks sticking to my face. "I'm so fucking sorry."

Gage's deep voice fills the room, and I force myself to open my eyes to look at him. "Put me down." My voice cracks with emotion. "Your words are empty, Gage."

I struggle against him until he finally relents and helps me to my feet. Tearing the saturated t-shirt over my head, I pay no attention to his shocked expression when it hits the floor with a loud slap. I grab a towel and wrap it around my body, leaving him in the bathroom alone. My head pounds from the pain of crying, but the ache in my heart hurts far worse. His words might have been said without thinking, but deep down I think there is some truth to them and that he's only helping me out of some sort of savior complex he has stemmed from the incident with his mother. He couldn't save her, so he'll do whatever he can to save me—his atonement in life. Well, I refuse to be anyone's project, especially when I have unrequited feelings for them.

Pulling on a pair of athletic shorts and a t-shirt that Archer delivered, I turn around to find Gage standing behind me. "Move."

"No." He backs me against the dresser, my back pressing into the wooden edge.

I press my hands against his chest and shove, trying to get out of his caged hold. "Listen to me, butterfly." He steps closer, forcing me to look up at him. His expression stops my feeble attempts to escape. Much like my own eyes, his are red. "I didn't mean what I said. I'm angry and I lashed out at you."

"Lashed out at me? That's rich, Gage. I'm just someone you're helping out. I'm sorry… but I'm pretty sure you said you cared about me—my mistake in thinking that meant something more than it did." My callous words stun him and I'm able to push under his arm. Not wanting to hear any more from him, I jerk open the bedroom door and disappear into the hallway.

Danny, who is standing in the kitchen when I step inside it, glances over at me. His eyes widen at my appearance. "You okay?" He glances at Gage, obviously standing behind me.

"Fine." I snap, jerking open the fridge to grab a bottle of water.

Gage steps toward me and I hold my hand out. "*Poppy*." His voice cracks with emotion, but I'm too pissed to give in.

"Right now, I don't want to talk to you—in fact, I'd rather not hear your voice. Words have power, Gage. And you chose poorly… anger or not." I step into his space and jab my finger into his chest. "I will not be *that* girl. Rest assured I won't make the mistake again—I received your message loud and clear. You're just helping me out. I won't expect us to share anything personal from here on out. Because your *careless* words have consequences." I step around him. "Excuse me."

I glance over at Danny, who is watching with a confused expression, and leave him standing speechless as I head out of the room. Needing a moment of air, I pull open the front door and step onto the front porch. The sky is black and depressing as it dumps rain in buckets across the landscape.

Grateful for the covered porch, I wander over to the corner and lean against the railing, staring out into the sky. The stars are absent from the storm clouds, the sky mimicking my emotions to a tee.

Deep down, I want to believe he didn't mean what he said, but the words hurt nonetheless. The ache between my legs is a reminder of what I gave him—of what he threw back in my face. My adult life has been nothing but control and dictated rules. For seven years I've been held prisoner in my own home, listening to men speak to me exactly the same way Gage did. Until now, their words did little to hurt me. Funny how one man eviscerated the barrier I have around my heart, only to treat me with just as little regard as them. The sound of footsteps has me taking a deep breath.

I'm not ready to face him because I know I'll throw myself into his arms despite being hurt by him. "Gage, I don't want to talk to you."

"Good thing I'm not Gage."

The familiar voice raises the hairs on my arms as I slowly turn around. "Eduardo." I lick my lips and lean against the wooden barrier. "How did you find me?"

"You really thought you could hide from us, Poppy?" His sinister laugh makes my gut coil with fear. "Doesn't matter. All that matters is I'm here to bring you home."

"No." I hold my arm out. "I'm not going with you." Wishing I hadn't come out here, I glance around, praying someone —*anyone*—sees what's happening. One of the neighbors happens to be climbing out of her car and glances up. She must register the terror in my eyes because I see her pull out her cell phone and hurry back inside. I pray to God she's calling the cops.

He steps forward, his arm lashing out so fast I don't have time to dodge him. "That's where you're wrong, puta. You don't have a choice."

He digs his fingers into my hair and jerks hard, causing me to hit the wooden slats. My knees, already tender from falling in the shower, throb with pain and I let out a painful cry.

"Stop... please."

12

Gage

"WHAT IN THE fuck did you do?" Danny folds his arms across his chest when the door slams shut.

Closing my eyes, I exhale the breath I'd been holding. "I said something I didn't mean."

"Yeah… I got that." Danny scowls at me. "And exactly what didn't you mean?"

Shaking my head, I pin him with a look that makes him bristle. "Did you know Archer put a gun in the duffle bag?"

"Yeah. So?" He narrows his eyes at me. "He felt it was necessary. Gage, I haven't told you yet, but the cat incident last night wasn't accidental."

I bristle at his words. "What do you mean?"

"It means I think it was a decoy. I've got this place locked down tight, but Archer felt you having a gun was smart."

"I don't do guns." I grit out through a clenched jaw. "He knows that. Not since..." I let my words trail off, not wanting to say them out loud.

Danny shakes his head. "Look, I get it. But you might need it. Still doesn't explain what you did to that woman out there."

I follow Danny into the living room. "She knew something was wrong and was trying to help. I—" I swallow the bile burning inside my throat. "When I pushed her away, she told me I didn't get to shut her out. And the dumb fuck that I am told her she didn't get a say just because I was trying to help her."

"Ouch." Danny looks toward the window. "Yeah... I can see why she's pissed. Did you mean that?"

"No. Of course not. I don't—" I take a deep breath. "It scares me to admit what she means to me. Because when I do, it's going to change everything."

He makes a clicking noise in the back of his throat. "Change how? Maybe make you less of a cold-hearted prick?"

I arch a brow at him and roll my eyes. Yeah—I get it. I'm known as the frozen-hearted doctor who won't commit to a woman. "Share myself with someone. Love is a foreign concept for me. Even *like* is a new emotion for me—love is not meant for Winston's. But seeing her hurt... *fuck,* it was a stupid mistake and now she won't talk to me."

"Make her... I have to admit, you distraught over a woman is not something I thought I'd see. At least not settling down with one. If you don't go out there and beg her to forgive you, you'll be a miserable prick."

"You're—" my words are cut off by the sound of a gut-wrenching scream.

Danny bolts past me, his gun drawn, and yanks the door open. Eduardo has Poppy by her hair and is trying to drag her across the porch. He doesn't notice Danny—he's too busy fighting *her*.

"Let her go or I'll pull the trigger." Danny presses the barrel of his weapon against Eduardo's head. Eduardo stiffens and slowly releases her hair. "And don't even think about reaching for your gun. I'm a bit trigger-happy—it's why I'm not a cop instead."

Eduardo thrusts his hands into the air. "You're making a mistake."

"Maybe… but you're not leaving here with that woman."

I'm rooted to the spot, unable to move. My brain flashes back to my mother lying on the floor with my dad holding the gun in his hand. It isn't until Poppy scoots herself into the corner of the porch's railing and whimpers that I snap from my frozen state and rush forward, unconcerned for the thug currently standing between us. All I care about is getting to her because I can't lose her—and that realization rocks me to the core.

As I reach her terrified frame, the sound of sirens registers in the distance, their flashing lights filling the once-darkened sky as they near. I whisper her name as I slowly squat in front of her. "Butterfly." Glancing behind me, I see the lethal glare Eduardo is giving me, but I don't care. The only thing that matters is the woman curled into a ball in front of me.

"I'm going to lift you, okay?" I reach out timidly, watching for any sign she doesn't want me to touch her. Poppy shocks me when she unfurls her body and launches herself at me. I clutch her against me and wrap my arms around her. "I got you."

Lifting her off the ground, I stand and carry her past Eduardo. His voice is like venom as he spits out, "You might have won now… but eventually, I'll get what's mine."

"She's not yours," I growl. "She's no one's."

I leave Danny alone with the piece of shit responsible for Poppy's torment and carry her inside. Not wanting to let her out of my arms, I sit down on the couch and cradle her against me. Her knees are scraped up and red, but that appears to be the only injury she has. Thank God. Had she been out there a moment longer with him—I hate to think about what would've happened. "Butterfly, can you look at me?"

Her head shakes as she buries it against my shirt. At least her shivering has stopped, but she still won't look at me. Brushing my hand down her hair, I press a kiss to the top of her head. "Fine. I'm going to talk for a minute."

I take a deep breath and blow it out. "What I said to you earlier was me being a chickenshit for so many reasons. I'm not used to sharing myself with anyone but my brothers— and even *they* don't get all of me. That doesn't excuse my words, though. You aren't someone I'm just helping, Poppy. You're so much more. This situation has me not knowing up from down and I stupidly lashed out at you, the one person who gets me better than I get myself. When I heard you scream—" I take a breath trying to quell my nerves. "I think my heart stopped. Seeing that motherfucker drag you across the porch with his gun aimed at you nearly broke me. All I could see was my mother the night my father killed her and thought to myself, 'you're losing someone else important to you'."

Poppy lifts her head, her eyes glistening with tears. "I'm scared." Her voice cracks and I follow the trail of a tear as it rolls down her cheek.

"I know, butterfly. But I swear we'll fix this. I won't let anything happen to you. Can you forgive me for my callous words earlier? I care about you—more than I thought possible."

She leans into me. "Yes." Her words are barely a whisper as she speaks. "I know you were just angry, Gage. But when you walked out of the bathroom—my heart hurt worse than anything I've ever felt before."

"God, I'm so sorry." I squeeze her against me. "I'm bound to fuck this up, Poppy. There has never been a woman I wanted as much as I want you."

"I'm sorry to interrupt." Danny closes the door behind himself. "But we have to leave."

Poppy stiffens in my arms at his words. "I'll grab our things." I move her to the couch and stand. "Wait here, Poppy. Danny, don't take your eyes off her."

"I'll come with." She starts to shift off the couch, but I lean down, bracing my arms around her. "I need to call my brother... and if you come with me, I'll be distracted. We don't have time for that, Butterfly. So *please* wait here." I press my lips to her forehead and hurry upstairs before I change my mind.

Grabbing the items from the bathroom, I set them on the dresser. Pulling the bag from the drawer, I pause, staring at the gun resting at the bottom. Looking at the cool metal, I realize I've been stupid to allow my demons to have control over me. I shove everything inside the bag and hurry to the bed. Sitting down on the edge, I grab my phone and scroll to find Drake's number. It's late, and tonight was the Gala, but I don't care. I need to tell him what's going on.

Drake's sharp tone filters through the line. "What?"

"I fucked up." I pinch the bridge of my nose and sigh. "Drake… this is—I fucked up."

"Gage. What are you talking about? The girl? You can bring her back here. Stay in a sanctuary apartment if you want."

Shaking my head as if he can see me, "Hugo knows where we are." I take a deep breath before continuing. "Eduardo found us tonight. The police have arrested him. Where are you in getting this thing finalized?"

Drake growls into the phone. "Fuck, Gage… I just filed last week. Hugo paid me a visit and I can tell you this will not be easy. Call Archer. Tell him what's going on and let him assess the situation."

"I'm sure Danny will, if he hasn't already." I breathe out another heavy breath. "I'm sorry, Drake. I didn't mean to cause problems like this… but this woman—" I pause, unable to articulate my feelings to him.

A sigh of his own slips out. "I think I get it, Gage. Just… be careful. Okay? Your life is more important than a woman you barely know, and Hugo isn't someone to fuck with."

"My life means nothing anymore… we were wrong, Drake. So fucking wrong." Poppy steps into the room, her eyes uncertain as she steps toward me.

"I'm sorry. I know you said to wait, but Danny is tied up on the phone and I was afraid to be alone."

I reach my hand out to her and tug her toward me. "I gotta go. I'll call Archer." The phone drops beside me as Poppy straddles my lap. "God, you're beautiful." I brush aside the loose hair around her face. The bruising around her nose has started to fade and the redness that once tinted the whites of her eyes has nearly vanished. I want to kill the motherfucker for putting his hands on her the way he did.

"Danny said we're going somewhere else. I hate this." She bites her lip, glancing away. When she turns to face me, I watch as her eyes flick to the duffle on the floor. "Why do you have rope in the bag?"

"What?" I blink in confusion, not at all expecting her question.

"I saw the rope in the bag, Gage. What's it for? Were you planning on tying me up so I didn't go back to Alessandro?"

Growling as I stand, my fingers grab the handle and I jerk it off the floor. Slinging it over my shoulder, I shove my cell into my pants. My fingers grip her chin and I lift her face to peer into her eyes. "You weren't supposed to see that, Butterfly. I told you that I had lived a life doing things that would make you blanch. I didn't request the rope, but I will tell you this much. If I were to use it to tie you up, it would be for both of our pleasure." Glancing at my watch, I wince when I see how much time has already passed. "But it's late, and this discussion isn't one we have time for. Let's get moving." I swat her ass as she steps in front of me.

"Fine… but at some point, we're going to talk about this."

13

Gage

DANNY HASN'T SAID MUCH. In fact, he hasn't spoken at all, which has me worried. "Is there something you aren't telling me?"

He glances into the rearview mirror, his eyes flicking to Poppy briefly. "I found the cat from last night around back this morning after the cops left." His gaze holds mine in the mirror, watching me. "It was mutilated—pretty sure it was a message left by Eduardo. Of course, he thought he'd take her, and we'd find it later. Kind of his way of saying fuck you to us."

"Jesus Christ." I wipe my palm down my face. "If he'd have taken her—"

"There's more." Danny sighs. "Eduardo made bail."

"*Fuck*." I mutter, stroking her hair as she lays against me in the car's backseat. "How the fuck is that possible? I was hoping he wouldn't get out for days—maybe buy us some time. But it's barely been three hours, and he's walking around a free man already?"

"Alessandro has plenty of people on his payroll, including cops, Gage." He glances back at me again before returning his eyes to the road. "Which is why we're getting you out of town."

This isn't exactly what I wanted, but it's no surprise Archer would want to put distance between us and Poppy's shitty family. "Where are we going?"

"Some friends have agreed to put you up in one of *their* safe houses."

I lean forward, peering into the still-darkened sky. "We've been driving forever, Danny. A little hint?"

"Look." He turns on his signal for the exit. "This guy knows his shit. He's former military—a friend of Archer's. The private security company he owns agreed to do this as a favor. You'll be staying at a cabin somewhere in Alabama until we can work out the rest of this shit storm."

We drive a few more miles before Danny finally pulls off the road and navigates the car down a long dirt driveway. The property opens to a large cabin hidden by the massive trees that look to be over a hundred years old. "This is it."

Danny kills the engine and slides from his seat. "Wait here."

The sun is starting to peek above the horizon, casting the early morning clouds into an orange glow that glitters across Poppy's skin. "Butterfly." I whisper her name, pressing a kiss to her head. "Wake up, we're here. Wherever the hell that is."

She shifts in my hold and pushes herself to a sitting position. Her eyes scan the area, finally stopping on me. "I've really fucked up everyone's life, haven't I?"

Poppy's still struggling with the blame. She can't seem to realize she isn't the cause of this—not really. Her twisted stepbrother and his asshole friends are the ones responsible for our current situation and *her* past one. They've been allowed to rule things with no consequences, and it's high time someone changed that. I pause, staring at her dejected expression, and think about my words carefully. Because what I'm about to say to her is important. I've never spoken the words I'm about to—and that scares me.

"Poppy." I shift so our legs are touching. "What's happening is no fault of your own. Do I wish circumstances were different right now? Yes. But if this was the only way for me to meet and have you come into my life, then I'll stay locked in this cabin with you indefinitely. I don't know what tomorrow brings, but for now, I'm going to focus on today." I see Danny waving his hand, signaling for us to get out. "For now... let's just live in the present. Okay?" My hand presses against her cheek, and she closes her eyes. "Danny is losing his shit. Let's go see what this place has to offer."

I climb from the car and hold my hand out to pull Poppy to her feet. A wave of exhaustion hits me, and my balance wavers for a moment. The shudder doesn't go unnoticed by her.

"When was the last time you slept well?"

"Meh." I wave her off. "I slept far less when I was in med school and interning at the hospital. This is child's play."

She jerks my hand, halting our movement forward. "I don't care, Gage. You haven't slept for more than an hour or two straight. When we get settled inside—please lie down... for *me*."

"We'll see. Let's find out what our home away from home is going to be like." Lacing my fingers with hers, I walk us over to the massive front porch where Danny is standing with another man. "Gonna tell us where we are now?"

The gentleman standing beside him is as formidable as Danny, and I tense when I see the way his eyes trail over Poppy's body. "Mr. Winston." He thrusts his hand out toward me, which I take despite the fact I want to punch him for ogling her. "I'm Michael Perez, personal security specialist."

"Gage Winston." I glance between the two men, waiting for further explanation. When I don't get one, I glare at Danny. "Archer isn't going to meet us here?"

"Mr. Winston." Perez interrupts. "Archer believed you would be safer being off the radar of your brother's company. He reached out to me, knowing I would do a better job of concealing your location."

"Better job? That's not possible." I grunt at him, knowing Archer is one scary motherfucker. There aren't many who I trust to take care of my safety. This Perez character dismissing him as being incapable pisses me off.

He smirks as he cocks his eyebrow at me. "Archer and I were in the military together. I'm by no means saying he isn't capable; he is. But what he *can't* do is keep her brother from paying someone to tell him where you are. Danny will remain here with you, making Archer the only other person to know your location." Perez holds my gaze. Poppy doesn't have a phone, because we left it on the hospital bed when we hightailed it out of there, and Danny confiscated mine before we left the last location, which now makes sense.

"Is that why you took my phone?" I cut my eyes to him, and he nods.

Shrugging his shoulders, he says, "I tossed it into the woods behind the other house. That way, if they're tracking your phone, they're gonna have a fun hike."

It slowly hits me. That means I won't be making any phone calls—to anyone. "Not even my brothers?"

"*Especially* your brothers. We've notified your employer that you won't be returning."

Poppy gasps beside me, jerking her hand free, and pushes past Danny. She practically runs up the stairs, shoving through the front door and slamming it behind her. "Fuck." I blow out a frustrated breath. "She thinks everything that happens is her fault, and now she'll blame herself for my untimely resignation."

"It's for the best. If your job doesn't know where you are... they can't be bought. If your brothers don't know where you are, they can't be coerced into telling anyone, either."

"Fine. How long will we be here?"

"As long as it takes." Perez turns toward the steps. "Come inside and we'll go over everything. One of my guys will be here with Danny—Hunter Gresham. He's recently out of the military and a scary motherfucker. He'll be here later to replace me."

I wonder where the hell everyone is going to sleep until we step inside. The outside does not do this place justice. A massive living room greets us as soon as we're through the door. The kitchen is situated toward the rear of the house, beyond the living space. A set of stairs leads to a second floor, where I assume the bedrooms are.

"Will we all be sleeping upstairs?"

Danny snorts, "Um. No—thank God. Seeing how you look at her, I imagine we won't want to be within hearing distance of *your* sleeping quarters. I am happy to say we, meaning Hunter and I, will sleep down here. There's a bedroom off the kitchen that allows us to hear everything that comes in and out of the house. Plus, the security monitors are in there. Since we'll take shifts guarding the house, only one bed is necessary."

My eyes narrow on him for a moment. "I'd appreciate it if you would censor your words in front of Poppy. I don't need her hearing you make assumptions about what's going on between us." The last thing I need is for her to think I want to bed her—even if I do.

"You mean you don't want to blow your chance? I don't blame you. Speaking of Poppy." Danny glances over his shoulder toward the steps. "You should go find her. We need her here when we discuss what to expect while we're cohabiting together."

Frowning as my voice takes on an almost whiny tone, I finally reach the end of my rope and complain, "Can it wait? I'm dead on my feet and would rather get some sleep so I can fully comprehend what you tell us. Right now, I'm not even sure I'm awake."

Danny nods his head, silently conveying a message to Perez. Normally I'd be pissed at the covert attempt to keep something from me, but I'm too fucking tired to care.

"Yeah. Hunter and I can cover everything with you later. He'll be bringing you some more clothes. I'll grab your duffle bag and drop it in the hallway outside your room."

"Thanks for doing this, Perez. I'm sorry we're meeting under these circumstances." I head up the steps, wondering what I'll find when I locate Poppy.

The first two rooms are empty, leaving a door at the end of the hall closed. Gripping the knob, I turn it slowly, relieved when I find it unlocked. Much like the rest of the house, this room is not what I expect. It has a large wrought iron framed canopy bed that's pushed against the wall. A chaise lounge is situated at the foot of the bed, still leaving plenty of space to move around. Scanning the room, I'm momentarily confused when I see it's empty—until I hear muffled crying coming from beyond a closed door.

Assuming it's the attached bathroom, I walk to it and pull it open. Poppy is seated on the closed toilet lid, crying. "Seems the bathroom is your hiding place, Butterfly."

Her reddened eyes meet mine. "I didn't want anyone to hear me."

Stepping in front of her, I hold out my hand. "Enough of this pity party. Let's go lay down before I fall over."

Reluctantly, she takes my hand and lets me pull her up. "Gage —" I press my finger over her lips, halting whatever apology she was going to spew.

I'm done letting her take the blame for this mess. I made a conscious decision to take her from the ER and protect her. She cannot continue to hold on to this guilt... I won't let her.

"Stop." I pause in front of the bed. "I do not want to hear another apology, or you say this is your fault. I took you out of the hospital. You didn't ask." I kneel in front of her and hook my thumbs into her black leggings, slowly squatting as I tug them down. "I knew there would be a consequence for doing it." Leaning forward, I press a kiss to her belly before slowly standing, dragging my fingertips across the surface of her skin as I do. "And as I told you, Poppy, I don't *need* to work. It was something I chose to do so I could make a difference in a world that didn't seem to care if I existed or not. And it can wait. Right now, making sure you're safe is all that matters."

Her eyes glisten with unspent tears. "I don't deserve your kindness."

"You're right. You deserve so much more." My lips cover hers in a demanding kiss.

Poppy flattens herself against me, her breasts poking through the thin cotton material against my chest as her arms wind around my neck. Her delicate fingers tug at my clothes, silently begging for me to strip with her. Giving in, I step out of our embrace and peel my shirt over my head.

After tossing it to the floor, I step around her and pull the covers back. "Climb in, butterfly."

Poppy slides into the bed, watching my every move as I shuck my pants. I keep my boxers on out of necessity, because without them, I'm not sure if I'd hold on to my self-control long. I slip in beside her, holding my arm out, as Poppy wiggles against me. "Normally I need complete darkness to sleep, but I'm so fucking beat, I don't think it's going to matter." I yawn, my eyes drooping as mutter the words.

"Sleep, Gage. You've earned the right to rest." She presses a kiss to my chest.

Even the feel of her warm lips against my chest has my cock stirring, despite my exhaustion. He apparently doesn't care that

I'm one breath away from a sleep coma. Poppy's hand drifts over my abdomen, stopping at the top of my boxer's elastic band. "How can you be turned on when you're about to pass out?"

"Everything about you turns me on, butterfly. My cock doesn't care if my eyes are begging to be closed—not when you're this close." She whimpers, shifting her body against me nervously. "Ignore it, Poppy. It's just a stupid dick and it'll go down once I fall asleep."

"I've never..." She buries her head into my armpit.

Not sure what she is trying to say, I glance down at the top of her head. "You've never what?"

"I'm—" Her voice cracks as she peeks up at me.

My chest constricts, and my freeze understanding dawns on me, and I blink in shock. "Are you a virgin, Poppy?"

"Yes." Her eyes find mine as I reach over and turn on the bedside lamp. "It's the only thing I've been able to keep for myself. And Alessandro was clear that if he couldn't have me...no one could until I was married."

I'm completely stunned that she's untouched. How is it this beautiful woman is still a virgin? I try to move away, but Poppy grabs my arm. "Please don't." She growls. "Don't you dare be like them and make fucking decisions for me. I'm not some stupid little girl who can't think for herself."

Turning my gaze to hers. "Poppy..." I growl her name. Just the thought of her untouched pussy has my dick hardening even more. She slides her fingertips beneath the waistband of my boxers, the tips of her fingers grazing my cockhead. I hold myself perfectly still, unsure of what to do. Knowing she's a virgin does something to me, I can't explain. Something visceral burns in my blood, heating my body with a need I don't think I can contain anymore.

I roll us over, pinning Poppy beneath me and growl. "I don't do soft, Poppy. I'm not a man who does relationships. Sex for me is a means for pleasure only—*my* pleasure." I close my eyes and take a deep breath. My control is waning and I'm seconds from tearing through her innocence. "Once I sink my cock into your pussy... no other man will touch you again. The only thing stopping me from taking what I want right now is the exhaustion."

I quickly roll over and flop on my back, willing myself to control the monster threatening to tear into her. "Just go to sleep, butterfly. This is not the time to push for things you're not ready for."

She presses her hand against my chest, and I can feel her staring at me. Cracking one eye open, I peek at her and smile. Apparently, my words have shocked her, or it's harder for her than for me to ignore the raging boner I have. Either way, I'm not prepared for what she does. Poppy slides out of my arm and pushes my boxers down, exposing my very stiff member.

"Popp—" My words die and my mind blanks. For a minute, I wonder if I'm asleep and this is a dream, but the intense suction around the crown of my shaft has my hips jerking. "Oh, *fuck*."

"Just lay there and let me take care of you." Poppy returns her hot mouth to my cock.

I've done a lot of kinky shit in my thirty-seven years, but the simplicity of her deep throating my dick is unlike anything I've ever experienced. Her hand works in tandem as her head bobs along the throbbing rod. She's like a magician, weaving her magic around my body with each lick. When she cups my balls in her hand, I groan in satisfaction. My body is on the cusp of exploding—but I'm not ready to end this pleasure. I fist the sheets and will myself to take some steadying breaths. However, the minx laying across my pelvis has other plans. Her hand slips from around the base of my shaft and drifts back to my sack. I assume she's about to massage them, instead her fingers probe the tiny ring beneath them.

As I'm about to ask her what she's doing when she pushes her fingers into her mouth and then eases them inside my hole. She leans up, gripping my cock with her free hand, and shifts her head to look at me. As her tempo increases, her fingers root around in my ass until she finds what she's looking for. Electricity zings through my veins as she presses down on my prostate. Like a nuclear bomb detonating, my body seizes. My eyes roll into the back of my head, and I cry out, the force of my ejaculate expelling into her mouth like an automatic rifle going off.

"*Poppy*." I manage to moan her name as my body shuts down —the sound of her name on my tongue is the last thing I hear before the world fades to black.

14

Poppy

I WATCH in complete satisfaction as Gage cries out my name and fills my throat with his cum. His orgasm is powerful, and it takes everything in me to swallow all of his seed down without choking. I might be a virgin, but I'm definitely not inexperienced. While I refused to have sex with Eduardo or my stepbrother, Alessandro, they still had needs. Needs I learned to take care of whether I wanted to or not.

As far as sucking a cock—I learned quickly it was the only way to avoid a beating. Eduardo schooled me on how to do it properly, even down to the prostate massage. At first, I was mortified at the thought of shoving my fingers in a man's asshole, but when I learned it rendered him unconscious afterward, I became a pro. It was the only way to avoid him having his hands on me after.

Knowing how he needed sleep, I used my mouth for the greater good. Not like sucking his dick is a hardship—it did what I'd hoped... sent him into unconscious oblivion. The bad thing is, I'm left aching for his touch. I glance at him, smiling when I see the relaxed lines of his face in sleep. After cleaning him up, I tug the sheet over his body. He's so out of it, he doesn't feel me move off the bed. I'm too wound up to join him, so I tug my clothes back on and ease out of the room. When I get out into the hallway, I hear muffled voices downstairs.

As soon as I step into the living room, Danny, and a man I don't recognize, stop talking and turn to face me. "Ms. Jefferson, is everything alright?" Danny furrows his brows in concern.

"Yeah. I'm not tired and didn't want to disturb Gage—he needs to sleep."

Danny's expression softens and he motions for me to sit down. "Have a seat. Michael, this is Poppy Jefferson. Poppy—meet Michael Perez."

"Um." I glance over at the man, who is staring at me with a look that makes me bristle. "Hi." Perez keeps staring at me, and I shift nervously on the couch.

Danny must sense my unease because he fills the silence with more information. "He's with HIPs, a private security company here in Alabama."

"Alabama?" I blink, shaking my head. "I forgot we weren't in Georgia anymore. So, Mr. Perez—"

He cuts me off. "Just Perez, ma'am."

"Then call me Poppy, Just Perez." That gets me a sheepish grin, and I can't help but smile back, feeling some of the tension evaporating as I do. "You're going to be protecting us?"

"Not me directly, but one of my men. He'll be here soon." He looks back over at Danny, who seems to be studying me. "He and Danny will stay with you until Gage's brother can make headway with your protective order. Though—"

"It's a piece of paper and won't stop him from hurting me or Gage." I finish, not needing him to tell me what I already know. "Have I condemned him to a life on the run?"

I fight back the urge to cry, knowing my tears won't change anything. Danny cocks his head toward Perez, and they share a silent conversation before Perez speaks. "I think it will come to a head. It's going to end one way or another."

"You mean someone will get hurt." I state the unsaid meaning in his words. "Why does my life have to be so fucking difficult?"

"Can I ask you a question?" Perez leans forward, resting his elbows on his knees as he looks at me. Giving him a slight nod, he takes a deep breath and purses his lips before speaking. "Have you considered changing your identity?"

I had, but until now, I had no means of escaping my stepbrother or his cronies. "Until this moment, I had no way of getting out of his sight. He kept someone on me at all times. The few times I slipped away from his guards were when I went to the park for a run. But even then, they knew a general idea of where I was."

"But now you can do exactly that. My company can help you start over. A new name, a new appearance—a new life."

I ponder his words, wondering if that's the thing to do. "Wouldn't he find me, eventually? His reach is far greater than you realize."

Perez flicks his eyes at Danny for a moment before settling back on me. "We'd stage your death, Poppy. We're not stupid in thinking that just a simple identity change would keep you safe. This isn't our first rodeo with making someone disappear."

"That would mean leaving *everything* behind, right?" I didn't have to say Gage. Their shared glance tells me they know exactly what I'm insinuating.

"Yes." He stands at the sound of a car door slamming outside. "That'll be Gresham. Look, I don't expect you to know what you want right this second, but think it over, Poppy. This situation isn't going to get easier. It's going to get worse— much worse."

Perez excuses himself, leaving me alone with Danny. "What would *you* do?"

Danny blows out a breath. "If it was the difference between protecting those I love and potentially losing everything— walking away is the right thing to do to make sure they were safe. This isn't going to be an easy decision. Normally, I'd encourage you to have this conversation with Gage, but I know what he'll say. He'll tell you not to go."

"And how do you know that?"

"Because if I had a woman like you, I would tell her the same thing. I would burn down the world to keep her, rather than risk losing her in any way."

I watch him stand and head into the kitchen, leaving me with his words. Words that hit me straight in the chest, filling me with uncertainty and a hollow feeling. The thought of walking away makes my skin itch like I've just rolled around in an ant bed, yet I don't want to risk anyone being hurt.

"I'll be outside," I call out to Danny in the kitchen, who simply grunts an unintelligible response.

Pushing to my feet, I go in search of Perez. There are questions I need answered, because right now, I'm more confused than ever. I find him outside with a man that has me nearly tumbling down the steps. He's beyond gorgeous—but not an 'in your face' kind of handsome. He's a little taller than Gage, with the same brown hair. Except his hair is shaved like someone who's in the military might wear it. He turns his gaze on me and quirks an eyebrow at my bumfuzzled expression. Perez cuts his eyes in my direction and shoots me a knowing smile.

"Yeah... all the ladies look at him the same way—don't feel bad." He chuckles as he waves me over. "Poppy, meet Hunter Gresham. Hunt." He turns to the muscular man. "This is Poppy Jefferson."

"Nice to meet you, Ms. Jefferson."

I blink, words failing me. It's not like I want to get in his pants, but damn, he's attractive and right now I seem to have forgotten the basic skill of speaking. "Right... yes," I mutter, turning my attention to Perez, who is currently trying to hide his bemused expression. "Sorry to intrude, but I wondered if I could ask you some questions before you go."

"Sure." He leans against the car. "What do you want to know?"

My gaze flicks at Hunter, who is watching us with curiosity, and I hesitate. "Um... If I took you up on the offer you made inside, how quickly would it happen?"

"A week."

"And could I tell Gage what was happening or would I just suddenly—" My hands flap around in the air as I try to find a tactful way of asking.

Perez fills in the blank. "Die?"

Hunter smirks when my eyes widen at his direct response.

"Um... yeah, that."

Perez pushes off the car and starts toward the driver's side. "Unfortunately, 'sudden' is the only way to make everyone believe it—so no... Gage would not be aware of your untimely death in advance. Poppy?" He pulls open the door and pauses. "—You don't need to decide today. Let's see how this thing plays out first."

"I think I want you to prepare for the inevitable... in case something else happens. As much as it kills me to think about walking away before he and I have had a chance—" I swallow the bile burning in my esophagus. "Him getting hurt or killed because of me would be far worse than knowing he's alive and I just can't have him."

Perez tilts his head at me. "You sure about that, Poppy?"

Closing my eyes, I force out the words, which are barely a whisper. "Yes." When I open them, he is staring at me with such intensity, I know he doesn't believe the lie I just told—because I don't believe it either.

"I'll be in touch." Perez climbs into the car, and I watch as he pulls out of sight.

"Let's go inside." Hunter's voice cuts through my trance and I turn to find him scanning the grounds. "Even though we're off the grid, being out in the open isn't smart."

I roll my eyes and head toward the porch. "Bossy, I see."

Hunter chuckles behind me. "My fiancée says the same thing."

"I'm sure she likes it." I quip, stepping inside to find Danny sitting on the couch.

His confused expression pauses on Hunter, then looks at me. "Who is *she?* And what does *she* like?"

"Hunter's fiancée. Apparently, she's okay with his *bossy* side." I throw myself onto the opposite end of the couch and let out a frustrated huff.

Hunter sits down in the chair opposite Danny and grins. "I never said she liked it. *You* did. Besides, she makes my *bossy* nature look like child's play. You lucked out, drawing me for your guard. She would have locked you in your room."

I shoot him another glare and then smile. "Whatever."

"Did you get your questions answered?" Danny diverts my attention back to him. My mouth hangs open at his ability to know why I went outside. "It was all over your face, Poppy. Perez offered you a lifeline, and you needed to get more information."

"Yeah… I did. But it didn't really help me know what to do."

"Starting over can be scary, but I seriously doubt you'd be alone long. You're a knockout and could have any man you want."

"The man I want is currently upstairs, dead to the world," I grumble, pissed off at no one in particular.

Danny shrugs his shoulder, not sure what to say. Hunter, however, stands. "He could always 'disappear' with you."

While the thought is tempting, I would never ask him to give up his family for me—a woman he's only known for a few weeks. "That's not an option. I can only hope his brother works magic and makes this mess disappear. Because my gut tells me someone's heart isn't going to come out of this unscathed."

If I leave, Gage's heart will be broken. If I stay and something happens to him, mine will. There doesn't seem to be a solution on the horizon. Maybe I should just go back to Alessandro and convince him to leave Gage alone if I marry Eduardo. Of course, that would cause two broken hearts, anyway. But at least we'd both be alive. Maybe.

"How about for now, we watch a movie? Hunter is going to walk the house and secure the perimeter and after that, we'll eat some dinner. Hopefully Gage will be awake, and we can give y'all the rules." Danny kicks his feet up on the table and clicks on the TV.

Hunter has disappeared out the door, leaving me to stare at the big screen. I don't have a clue what Danny puts on to watch, because all I can think about is how in the fuck I'm going to unravel this knotted rope I call my life.

There must be a solution… one where everyone wins.

15

Gage

I'm less than thrilled that the bed is empty when I finally wake up. I have no idea how long I've slept, but I feel a thousand times better. After relieving myself in the bathroom, I brush my teeth with the toothbrush I find and tug on my pants. Padding out of the room barefoot and shirtless, I stop at the bottom of the steps when I hear the sweetest sound— Poppy's laughter.

She's standing next to Danny in the kitchen, stirring something on the stove. A rage like nothing I've ever felt comes over me when I watch her hold the spoon out to him, and he leans in to flick his tongue across whatever she's cooking. Without thinking, I stride into the kitchen and yank her against me. The spoon clatters to the floor, causing Danny to jump back and gape at me.

"Gag—" I don't let her finish her words. I toss her over my shoulder and storm out of the room.

"What the hell, Gage?" She hits my backside as I climb the steps. "Put me down, you ass."

I'm too worked up to respond. Seeing her with Danny, though innocent, triggered something inside me. This woman is mine and I'm about to show her exactly what that means. Slamming the bedroom door, I toss her on the bed. Her eyes widen as she watches me move around the room.

The voice in the back of my mind is telling me to take this slowly, but the beast inside me is screaming to take what I've denied myself. It took sheer willpower to not fuck her senseless earlier when she confessed to being a virgin. I wanted nothing more than to roll over her and plunge my aching cock into her untouched pussy—but I didn't. And now I plan to mold her body with my cock.

"Poppy… you're burned into my veins. Nothing will come between me and something I want. Your *step*brother might be ruthless… but so am I. Especially when I want something as badly as I want you."

"You say that as if you *own* me." I watch as she blinks back the hurt in her eyes. "I don't want to be owned by anyone ever again."

Pushing her back onto the bed, I ease myself between her legs and pin her body beneath me. I lean forward, a breath separating our mouths, and search her eyes. Her breath hitches as I run my fingers down her arm and latch onto her hip. "The only thing I want to own is this." I slide my palm between her legs, cupping her sex. "And this." I trail my fingertips across her pelvis, tracing a path across her belly. My ascent continues as I push up the cotton shirt she's wearing and rest my palm between her breasts, splaying my fingers flat against her sternum. "I want to consume you as much as you consume me, butterfly. It's not ownership like property. It's ownership like *possession*."

My mouth covers hers and I thrust my tongue inside, demanding compliance. I push her hands above her head and pin them on the mattress with a slight grip. "I want to bury myself inside you so deep that you'll feel me there for years to come. I don't think you understand what you're doing to me. Everything about you pulls me in, making me want to fuck you until there is no doubt how much I want you. It's taking every ounce of willpower I have *not* to strip you bare and ruin you for any other man."

Slipping down her honey skin, I tug her pants down slowly, watching her for any sign it's too much. When she doesn't fight me, I pull the cotton material from her body and toss them to the floor—panties and all. Closing my eyes, I count to ten, reigning in the beast, begging to be let loose. As much as I want to lay claim to this woman, I don't want to hurt her. Spreading her thighs apart to expose the pink cleft, I groan when I see how wet she is for me. "Such a beautiful fucking sight."

I glance up and hold her gaze as my tongue darts out and drags through the glistening slit. "I imagine this is what it feels like when you take your first hit of drugs. Something so fucking delicious should be illegal, but it's not. Now you're the drug and I'm the addict, Poppy. No amount of rehab will rid my system of you."

She bites down on her lip, the muscles of her legs flexing beneath my hold. Pressing against the tops of her thighs, I urge them wider, needing better access to her sweetness. Flattening my tongue against her core again, I swipe it through her delicate lips, devouring her inside out. Her body responds, coating my face in her juice.

"I want you to cum hard for me, butterfly. Cover my face in you, so every man who sees me knows I've tasted heaven."

I dive in, pressing my nose against her clit, brushing it against the swollen bundle of nerves. My tongue darts in and out of her core, pulling her moans out louder and louder as she climbs toward her peak. Easing a finger inside, I push in as far as I can into her channel—she's so fucking tight and the sensation of how hard she clenches around my knuckle makes my dick ache with a need to be inside her. Pumping my wrist as I suck and bite on her clit, I feel her body as she begins to respond. Her walls flutter as her back arches off the bed.

"Oh fuck," she cries out, her body shuddering with a violent orgasm.

And as beautiful as she is falling apart, my cock pulsates with anticipation when I witness the stream of fluid that seeps out around my knuckle.

"Beautiful." I kiss her thigh, smearing the cream around her entrance as I move up her body. "Tell me no if you don't want this… because once we do, there's no turning back."

Poppy reaches up and presses her palm to my cheek. "I don't want to go back."

Losing all sense of reason, I press my cockhead between her folds. It might be the hardest thing I do, but I pause, giving her a moment to adjust to my size. Poppy whimpers beneath me, her eyes closing as I push into her painstakingly slow, inch by inch. She tenses beneath me from the sharp pain of her barrier giving way to my final thrust. There's only a momentary resistance signifying that I've erased the last hold she had on her innocence. I'm buried so deep, I'm pretty sure you can't tell where I start, and she ends. I give her time to adjust—even though I want nothing more than to tear into her like the savage beast I am. Instead, I pump into her with a tenderness I had no idea I possessed. Our bodies become fused in a haze of desire, and I have no doubt if I could crawl inside her and live there, I would. The feeling of her body wrapped around mine sends me into a state of euphoria and I wonder if I've actually died and gone to heaven for real.

She lets out a tiny mewl as her pussy contracts around my shaft. As she calls out my name, I swear I hear angels singing. I don't stop... *fuck*—I can't. It's like her body is electrified and I'm a magnet being drawn to the surface. The sound of skin slapping and her sexy whimpers are the only sounds filling the room. This woman has no idea what she's done to me, but I plan to show her by giving her every part of myself.

Poppy must sense my struggle to keep my thrusts slow and gentle because I feel her tense. "Gage... please."

I still, holding myself inside her. "Please what, Poppy?"

"I need..." I shift my body, grinding my cock into her. "Oh, God." Pleasure ripples through her and her body shudders as I continue to pump my hips.

Needing to feel closer to her, I prop myself on my elbows and press my lips to hers. I've broken so many rules tonight with Poppy. Taking her like this is a novelty for me, so much so I half expect a feeling of panic. But all I feel is a deep, unbridled connection to her. This is more than sex... this is the beginning of something I never saw coming.

The prickling awareness that I'm about to explode starts at the base of my spine. Needing her to fall into oblivion with me, I pick up my pace. "Can you come for me, baby?"

I shift my body so I can slip her leg around my hip and ease my hand between us. Circling her bud, I coax another orgasm from her. Her cunt tightens around my shaft in a grip that has me nearly blacking out. The force of her release is so powerful, I cry out and come undone. The heat of my seed fills her womb as we both let go.

As I slip my cock from her, I see the evidence of what I took from her. My cum is mixed with tendrils of red seeping out of her center and coating her thigh. Rolling from the bed, I hurry to the bathroom and wet a washcloth with warm water. There is an overwhelming need to tend to her, which is something I've never done with a woman—not like this, anyway. When I return to her, I take a moment to admire her flushed skin. The remnants of what we did seem to mock me from the inside of her legs, and I'm hit with the under-standing of what I forgot.

"Fuck... Poppy, we didn't use protection. I'm sorry, butterfly, I promise I'm clean." I wipe the mess from her body and toss the cloth to the floor before climbing into bed beside her.

She sighs against me. "I don't care. I'm on the pill."

I close my eyes and wait for the panic that doesn't come. I'm never this irresponsible—not after a mishap when I was younger that nearly cost me more than my soul. But with Poppy, anxiety is the furthest thing from my mind. Taking a deep breath, I release the breath I'm holding. "I've never been with a woman without a condom... but more than that—I never have intercourse with them in the traditional sense. You're the first woman in a long time I've let myself go with. I guess when I decided to make you mine, I lost my head. You seem to do that to me, butterfly." A soft chuckle escapes my lips. "Did I hurt you?"

"Wait." Poppy leans up and searches my face, her brows knit together in confusion. "If you didn't have intercourse... what did you do?"

My lips quirk into a grin because I forget how innocent to the ways of actual sex she is. "Anal or oral sex, Poppy. I would only fuck them in the ass or let them suck me off."

Her eyes widen and she buries her head in the crook of her arm and mumbles. "Oh."

"I swore I'd never take a chance on a woman trapping me. It got me off, and I made sure the women I was with left satisfied. It worked for everyone involved." Poppy shifts away from me, giving me her back. "Hey... why are you rolling away from me?"

"Why are you with me, Gage? You can have any woman you want—one without a psycho stepbrother and baggage."

I pull her against me, pressing my lips to her ear. "I don't want another woman... I want you, butterfly. You're the only woman my cock will ever be buried inside the way it just was. Stop thinking you aren't worth anything. Because to me, you're worth everything." I hold her tight, gently caressing her arm. My hand covers hers, and I lace our fingers together. "Let's get some rest. You're going to be sore after that."

"It was worth it."

16

Poppy

I SLIDE from the bed and tiptoe into the bathroom to relieve myself. Gage was right when he said I'd be sore—but it's in the most delicious way possible. After taking care of business, I splash some water on my face and swipe some toothpaste across my teeth using my finger. We still haven't unpacked our things, so there aren't any toiletries in here. Easing out of the bathroom, I note Gage sprawled out on the bed. His arm is tossed over his head and his body is spread out like a starfish, taking up most of the mattress. The early morning light casts an orange glow across his naked flesh, making me want to crawl back into bed and have my wicked way with him.

As I start toward him, determined to do just that, I see the duffle bag laying on the floor by the dresser. Curiosity gets the better of me and I find myself rifling through the contents. Paying no mind to the gun weighted at the bottom, my fingers wrap around the tan twine rolled into coils. I slip the two pieces of rope out and stare at them. His words come back to me—*You weren't supposed to see that, butterfly. I told you that I had lived a life doing things that would make you blanch. I didn't request the rope, but I will tell you this much. If I were to use it to tie you up, it would be for both of our pleasure.* Fisting the two coils in my hand, I stand and turn, startling when I find Gage's gaze locked on me.

"What are you doing, Poppy?" He's propped on his side against his elbow.

I hold out my hand. "Show me how you use this."

A strange emotion flickers across his face, but he covers it with a smile. "It's not important. Come back to bed."

"No." I stop a few inches from the mattress and toss the rope beside him. "I want to know what you meant at the other house."

He sighs heavily and shifts to sit up. "You're not ready for that, Poppy."

"Who are you to decide what I'm ready for? I'm not made of glass, Gage. You won't break me."

He stares at me—more like through me before he eases off the bed to stand. My skin pebbles with awareness as he stalks around me, pressing into me from behind. "And if I told you I love to see a woman coiled in rope as I give her pleasure, it wouldn't make you run?"

"You. Can't. Break. Me." My growl turns into a moan as his fingers slip down my front, landing on my wet center.

"If this becomes too much... tell me to stop." He licks at my ear, nibbling the soft flesh. "Say it, Poppy. I need to hear the words."

"Okay..." I whisper as he bites down on the crook of my neck and slides his fingers between my folds. *"Gage."*

"I need to see your beautiful ass, Poppy." He pushes me down onto the bed, gripping my hips in his hands. A moan slips out as he arches my backside up and dips his fingers inside me again. "Jesus, it's so warm. Do you like that I took your virginity?"

"*Please*." I beg, but for what, I'm not sure. I just know the fire I'm feeling right now can only be put out by him. I should be scared… but instead of fear, there's curiosity.

Withdrawing his fingers, I feel him part my cheeks. The sensation of his tongue hitting my slit has me pushing back into him, needing more. Gage must sense my silent plea because his face disappears from my core and I feel him pushing inside me. His fingers tangle in the strands of my hair and he pulls me back so we're both on our knees.

I'm lost to this man in more ways than I can count and it's a feeling I want to cling to, afraid I'll never have it again. Gage fastens his mouth over mine as he thrusts his dick in and out in a steady rhythm. His fingers cup my breasts, alternating between pinching my nipples and squeezing my heavy mounds. His tongue presses into my mouth, almost as if he's desperate to consume the very air I breathe. I swear it's like he's frantic to be inside my body and never come out. I feel a sudden loss when he slides out of me, but it's quickly replaced when he tugs me to stand and slams his lips over mine. As he steps back, my breath hitches at the look he's giving me. I've set the beast inside free, and from the looks of it, he wants to consume me.

Using his foot, Gage spreads my legs wide and steps closer to my body. Shoving me against the edge of the bed, I watch as he reaches around and grabs the rope I'd thrown at him. Biting down on my lip, I can't take my eyes off him. He pauses, glancing at me with concern. But I nod at him, silently telling him the only thing I feel is anticipation. He grips my hands, locking them together with one of his, and wraps the rope around my wrists, binding them together. Jerking them upright, he loops the twine over the top post of the canopy bed and jerks against the makeshift restraints. I don't miss the way his dick twitches against his abdomen. I assume from the anticipation of what we're about to do.

Using the remaining rope, Gage loops the twine ribbon around me, decorating my flesh with the hemp threads. Once he has it fashioned around my breasts, he steps back and admires me like I'm a piece of artwork meant to be in a gallery. "Fucking beautiful. Just like I expected."

"What is this, Gage?" I ask, mostly out of curiosity as I take in the woven design covering my chest.

Stepping forward, Gage grips my throat with his fingers and pulls my lips to his. There is so much he's saying with this kiss—it's heated with a neediness that I return without hesitation. An electric current races through my veins as he presses my hand to his cock. "No woman has ever gotten me this hard—and you're not even fully bound."

"Show me, Gage. Let me see you—all of you." My words come out breathy and needy.

He covers my mouth and sucks my tongue, tangling it with his. "I like the sight of ropes on a woman's delicate flesh. I like the feeling of control it gives me. But this—" He runs a finger across the binds. "—is something entirely different."

He bends down and grabs my feet, lifting my legs off the floor. "Hold on, Poppy." My hands reach out for the metal bar behind my head on instinct. "I'm going to show you what seeing you like this does to me. Hold on, butterfly... this is going to be turbulent."

Without another word, he slams into me. Gage's cock fills me completely, and he hisses at the sensation of how tight my insides grip hold of his shaft. He hasn't even moved yet, but that doesn't stop me from crying out. My body tenses from the invasion of his steel rod being driven into me with a savagery that borderlines insanity. I should tell him to stop, but I don't. Instead, I moan his name. Though the sound that comes out is more like a tribal chant to the gods as he pumps his hips back and forth with barbarity. At this angle, he's hitting me in the deepest of places, sending my body into the abyss with each stroke. I can feel the rope tightening around my chest with each thrust, but instead of pain, I feel pleasure. His fingers dig into my skin, biting at my flesh as sweat drips off his body. As he grinds his rock-hard shaft into me, I have no doubt he's scorching his soul as well as mine.

"Lock your ankles behind me." I do as he commands, and Gage slides his hand from my hip and presses his thumb against my bead of flesh. It's engorged, needing release nearly as much as I suspect he does. As soon as he pinches it between his fingers, he begs for me to join him in paradise. "I want you to come with me, Poppy."

I scream out, my voice getting louder with each thrust. I have no doubt what we're doing can be heard downstairs by the two men sharing the house with us—but Gage doesn't stop his relentless pace. I'm convinced he's turned on by the thought of them knowing how hard he's fucking me. I've created this possessive monster, and I don't regret a minute of it as he rocks into me with more force.

Just as my pussy locks down on his dick, I see his body tighten. Gage jerks wildly inside me, spilling his seed inside my womb. He pumps the last two spurts of his cum into me and pulls out, slowly easing my legs to the floor. My chest rises and falls as we both try to catch our breath.

Untying the binds from around my chest, Gage pulls my hands down, massaging the red marks as he guides me to the bed. Wordlessly, he lays me down and fetches a towel. After wiping me down, he climbs into bed beside me and nestles me against his chest.

"That was..." My words break through the silence, making him shift behind me. "Wow."

"I didn't hurt you, did I? I kind of lost control."

I press my hand over his. "There was nothing nefarious about what we just did. Will I be sore later? Probably. But it was worth it, Gage. I was serious when I said I won't break. I'm capable of telling you to stop or if something is too much. You don't—no, you won't hurt me. I trust you completely. I want to share every facet of your life with you... please don't hide yourself from me. I won't run."

Gage presses his lips to my neck and sighs. "I never thought I'd find myself here."

"What? On the run from a psychopath?" I laugh, knowing that's not what he meant.

He tightens his arm around me. "If being on the run is the only way to have *this*, then I'll run with you forever."

Gage laces his fingers with mine as my eyes grow heavy. Being in his arms feels like home, and I can only pray it isn't snatched away from me. Because while it's important for him to protect me—I feel the exact same for him. I would do anything to make sure he's safe... even if that meant walking away in the end.

Gage

I'M NOT sure if it's from the lack of consistent sleep over the last three days, or the vigorous athletics Poppy and I spent most of the night and early morning doing, but she and I slept until well after noon. We would have slept longer had her stomach not rumbled like an F4 tornado was barreling towards the house.

"Jesus... I guess that means you're hungry." I kick the covers off and press my feet to the floor. "It's already noon. I suppose we should head downstairs and take care of the alien living inside your stomach." And as if to make me look silly, my own stomach grumbles in agreement.

"I'm not the only one who needs food." Poppy quirks an eyebrow at me as she slips from the bed. Her curves are on display as she struts across the room toward the bathroom. "I need a shower—I don't want to go downstairs smelling like sex."

Stalking toward her, I grab her wrist and shift her back into the wall. "I kind of like you smelling like sex. It warns off other suitors."

Her palm presses against my cheek. "No need to warn them off—I'm pretty sure you've ruined me for other men."

I capture her lips with mine, enjoying how her body feels pressed against my own. "I think I need a shower, too." Scooping her off the ground, I carry us into the bathroom.

The shower is good in size, allowing both of us to fit inside the stall. The water blasts out cold, making Poppy jump in my hold. "Jesus." She shivers against me. "Maybe next time, warm up the water *before* we get inside?"

Giving her a wicked grin, I dig my fingers into her bottom and press her against the cool tile. "You'll forget all about the cool temperatures in a moment, butterfly." I ease my cock between her folds, relishing how her body flutters around my shaft.

This time when I take her, it feels different. For me, sex has always been a means to pleasure only. No feelings, no attachments. I've never kissed a woman during the act, and certainly never buried my dick inside her pussy. When I was just beginning medical school, I learned the hard way why you can't trust a woman. A girl I'd been casually dating told me she was pregnant—while I knew I'd always used a condom. I wasn't foolish enough to think they couldn't fail. The only thing was, she was expecting some grand gesture of marriage, or hell, serious commitment. Because, up until that moment, I hadn't realized she was in love with me. In the end, it came out that it was all a ruse to get me to marry her. From that day forward, I didn't fuck a woman in the traditional sense. It's also when I learned about the art of Shibari.

A few of my friends convinced me to join them at an exclusive club—a swingers club. At first I was reluctant, but when I roped Drake in to going along, I knew we'd found something that made the darkness we both felt burned through our blood abate. Then learning about rope play, and the power it gave me, was unlike anything I'd ever experienced. It became an integral part of my life and not one I can give up.

By the time we make it out of the shower, we're both famished. Poppy dresses in a pair of leggings and one of my t-shirts. Upon closer inspection, I realize it's not just any shirt– it's *the* shirt. The one I kept after the worst night of my life. After all this time, it's faded, and the threading is frayed around the sleeves, but the imprint of 'Pig Roast - APD Annual Charity BBQ' is still legible and I can't help but smile. Even in my darkest moment, this shirt felt like a lifeline. My fingers reach out as if they have a mind of their own and trace the cracked embellishment. Poppy glances over her shoulder and grins, unaware of the effect her wearing this shirt is having on me.

"I like my shirt on you... almost as much as I like it off." Poppy simply shakes her head as we come to a stop.

A man I don't recognize stands beside Danny in the living room, and I don't miss how his eyes trail the length of Poppy's body. She's oblivious to the look he's giving her, but it doesn't dampen the jealous monster I feel threatening to rear its ugly head. Granted, the last time *he* appeared, it led to my cock being buried inside her many times over.

"Hiya Danny, Hunter." So, the new guy's name is Hunter? I vaguely remember Perez saying he had someone else coming to guard us. "Hunter, this is Gage. He was asleep when you arrived."

Hunter dips his chin in greeting but doesn't say anything at first. "Thank you for being here." I force out the words even though I'd like to punch him in the face for the way he watches Poppy. "Hopefully it won't be for long if my brother has anything to do with it."

My eyes narrow and I pin him with a glare. He must realize how he's coming across because he suddenly shifts. "You two ready to talk over the logistics? We have some ground rules that we need to cover."

"Right to the point." I nod, sliding onto the couch as I tug Poppy onto my lap. "I like a man who's *professional* at all times." Poppy stiffens against me, obviously picking up on my semi-threatening tone. "Let's get to it—what can and can't we do while we're here?"

Hunter's eyes track my hands' movement as I brush my fingertips across Poppy's leg. Danny clears his throat, snapping us from the silent stand-off we're having. "Alright... first, let's start with basics. One of us, meaning me or Hunter, will always be awake. We'll likely rotate as needed. Now, the obvious. You can't leave the property for any reason. If one of you gets sick, we'll bring someone here if needed. Granted, we lucked out to have a world class physician here already." Danny grins, trying to lighten the tension in the room. He nods when only silence greets him. "Whew, okay. Tough room. We'd prefer you not to leave the house at all—but you can walk the perimeter or use the pool out back."

"Wait." Poppy interrupts, her head swiveling toward the back of the house. "There's a *pool?*"

Hunter chuckles at her response. "Yeah... *you've* only made time to see the bedroom."

Once again, she stiffens in my lap. "Do you have an issue I need to be made aware of?" My growl vibrates through the room, catching Danny off guard.

"Hunt." Danny shakes his head at him. "You need to relax, man. We're going to be here for an indefinite amount of time. You two being at each other's throats will make it unpleasant. And yeah—they've only seen the bedroom. Gage was running on three hours of sleep over a two-day period. Maybe you need to go call Allison and work out your shit. Stop taking it out on our charge."

Hunter closes his eyes and blows out a frustrated breath. "Fuck... I'm sorry, Mr. Winston, Poppy. I don't normally let my personal matters interfere with a job. Can we start over?"

"Who's Allison?" I grumble, irritated by everything at the moment.

Poppy turns halfway in my lap and presses her palm to my chest. "His fiancée." The knowing grin she gives me confirms she knows exactly what my problem is.

Rolling my eyes, I shift my gaze back to Hunter, who is still watching us. "Poppy's right. Allison is my fiancée. She's pissed that I took this job when we're due to get married in two months. Without knowing when it ends, she's worried we'll have to postpone."

"No," Poppy snaps. "There will be no more disruption to lives because of me—" My growl causes her to shoot me a narrowed glare. "Or my stepbrother. If need be, then we'll go to Plan B." I see Danny's eyes widen as he flicks them between us. "Shit." Poppy covers her face.

"What's plan B?" I tug her hand into mine, waiting for a response. When she makes no attempt to answer me and neither does Danny, I ask again. This time, my tone is a bit more demanding. "Poppy… what's *Plan B*?"

"She can't tell you." Hunter breaks the silence, glancing between me and Poppy. "Not unless you're willing to give up your family, sir."

"Explain. *Now*." I slide Poppy to the cushion beside me and pin Hunter with a glare that makes him bristle.

He looks at Danny, who seems equally uncomfortable. "We can't tell you—not unless you're willing to give up *everything*."

My head swivels in his direction and I narrow my eyes at him. "What do you mean—*everything*?"

"Everything. Your life, your family—all of it. If that's not something you're willing to do, then drop this conversation or you'll take away her chance at surviving if all else fails."

"I'm sorry." Poppy drops her head in defeat. "I wasn't thinking."

Hunter blows out a frustrated breath and starts toward the front door. "I'm going to walk the perimeter. You guys can figure this shit out."

"Gage—" Danny tilts his head and flicks his eyes to Poppy, who fidgets nervously beside me. "Please don't pressure her into telling you… because she'll cave. Just know it is an absolute last resort and we're going to do everything to make sure it's not needed."

The last thing I want to do is make her feel any more guilt or pressure, so I nod in agreement. In my gut, I know whatever the *plan* is, it's going to take her from me, and I don't like that feeling at all. Refusing to let it affect me, I grab the remote and lean back.

"How about we watch some television?" Poppy's head jerks up and her eyes find mine. "And maybe later, we can try out the pool."

Not being in control of this situation makes me feel inadequate. I *hate* how it makes her feel and despise the possibility being here may be all for nothing. Winding my fingers into her hair, I push down the fear brewing in my gut and settle onto the couch. I want to believe Drake will fix this situation, but the overwhelming feeling something big is coming for us lingers despite my attempts to pretend it's not.

18

Poppy

WE'VE BEEN HERE NEARLY a month with no word on my stepbrother. Gage and I have explored every nook and cranny of this cabin, and even make use of the pool as often as we can. For the first time in a long time, I feel somewhat safe. Too bad it's about to end.

But someone should've warned me concrete decks were this dangerous when wet. But I figure that out a moment too late as my body contorts and my foot slips out from under me. As my trajectory launches forward, I hear Gage scream my name. He lurches out of the pool a second too late and I hit the concrete. Perhaps this wouldn't be so bad on a normal day… but I'm holding a glass in my hand and instead of dropping the damn thing, I cradle it against my chest—that was mistake number one.

Mistake number two? Trying to get up on my own. In doing so, the glass embeds into my side, and I can't contain the scream that slips out. Gage is kneeling beside me, and despite the urge to pass out, I turn my head toward him.

"Fuck." I hear Danny's voice. "Let me get a towel."

"Butterfly, I'm going to roll you over." Gage's fingers grip my biceps and he somehow manages to roll me toward him. Hunter is on the opposite side, and I don't miss the horrified expression he's wearing. "Jesus."

Danny is back and I wince at the sensation of his hand pressing into my stomach. "Let's get her inside. Gage, what do you need?"

"Won't know until I get her inside—but at least something to get the glass wedge out."

His strong arms lift me up, careful not to jostle me too much, and he carries me into the house. "Shouldn't you d—do that out...ss...side." I manage to speak through the chattering of my teeth and the painfully shallow breaths I'm taking. "I... I'll...b–bleed... on the floor...."

Gage ignores my question and stalks through the backdoor. Hunter clears off the kitchen table with one swipe of his arm as Gage lies me down on the surface. "Hang tight, butterfly." He presses a kiss to my forehead and turns to Danny, who has carried in a first aid kit.

"It's a first responder kit—it's got Quikclot inside." He jerks open the top and hands something to Gage across my chest.

"Hold her down—this isn't going to be pleasant. Poppy, baby." Gage leans over and locks his gaze with mine. "I need to get the glass out."

Closing my eyes, I try to brace myself for the moment, but the burning fire that ripples up my side is worse than any blow I've ever suffered at the hands of my stepbrother, and I cry out. Hunter grabs my hand, trying to offer some comfort, but the pain is too much, and I waver on the edge of unconsciousness. I'm vaguely aware of the pressure in my gut before Gage covers my abdomen with a towel.

He grunts in frustration. "The wound needs more than I can do here, and she probably needs a dose of antibiotics. Unless you can get me a surgical-grade suture kit and a week's worth of, at minimum, Amoxicillin, and a decent painkiller, she needs a hospital, Danny."

"Fuck," he mutters, "you know that's dangerous."

"So is fucking with sepsis. I can't just snap my fingers and make this better. I'm a fucking amazing doctor—but not without the proper tools. I'm sorry, Danny, but she needs more than I got…"

"I'll be fine," I mutter through the tears falling at free will. "Just clean me up."

Gage presses his hand to my forehead. "No, Poppy. Even *if*… and that's a *big* if… I could get this wound closed—I can't risk an infection. That glass went in deep and the injury needs to be properly checked. Who knows how clean the glass was. And what if it nicked your spleen? Then the healing process gets complicated even more. Please don't argue, butterfly."

Danny mumbles something to Hunter. "Fine. Fuck, this is bad—Hunter, you take her, and I'll stay back with Gage. I need to call Perez and let him know."

"No. I'm going with her." Gage growls as his hand laces with mine. "I'm not letting her out of my sight."

"It's too dangerous, Gage. I'm sorry, but that's a hard no. Hunter is *trained* to do this. Just like you can assess that this is out of your capabilities here, I can assess that this is *within* his. He'll keep her safe—otherwise, she isn't going." I watch as a silent standoff happens before Gage seems to relent.

His strong arms lift me again, carrying me through the house. "You better not let her out of your sight."

"I won't. I'll guard her with my life."

I grip Gage's shirt. "Can someone get me some clothes?"

"You'll just ruin them, baby. No one cares that you're in your swimsuit." His lips press against my head as he slides me into the backseat. "Drive fast, but safe. She can't buckle properly."

Gage leans in and kisses me again. "I love you, Poppy. Come back to me, okay?"

My eyes widen at his words because it's the first time he's uttered them to me. "It takes me skewering myself to get a declaration of love?" I half chuckle, half gasp. "It's nothing a few handy dandy staples won't fix."

Gage brushes my hair back and slides out of the car. "Gage?" I whimper as he starts to close the door, halting him in place. "I love you too."

His eyes twinkle and I see him take a steadying breath as he dips his chin and steps back. Hunter nods at him as the door closes and I wince when the car starts to move. "You okay back there?"

"Fucking great." I close my eyes and breathe through the pain. It's lessened some, but every bump in the road is like being stabbed all over. "All I wanted was a freaking drink. This is just my luck."

Hunter chuckles from the front seat. "You're lucky it wasn't worse."

The fight to stay awake leaves me and I close my eyes. It isn't until a gust of air caresses my skin that I open my eyes to find a woman in scrubs at my open door. "Hey honey, we're going to get you out, okay?"

I mumble my approval as Hunter slips around her and eases me out. He lays me down on the gurney parked beside the car and follows us inside through a set of automatic doors. The smell of antiseptic assaults my senses and I blink at the sudden brightness of the fluorescent lights.

"Sir, someone will escort you to the waiting room." The nurse glances at Hunter, who visibly stiffens.

He grabs my hand. "I'm her husband—I can't leave her."

They push me into a small room, "I'm sorry… there isn't enough room in here. Please—I'll come get you when we're done."

Hunter is ushered out of the room, and a flurry of activity begins. An IV is jammed into my arm and someone starts cleaning the area that is still leaking blood. "Can you tell me what happened?"

An older man leans down eye-level with me and I begin recounting my clumsiness. I'm not entirely sure he believes me, but he goes back to assessing the gaping hole in my side. I feel a few pinpricks, then a burning sensation as he probes the wound.

"I'm going to have someone bring in the portable ultrasound so I can check you better. I want to make sure it didn't nick anything vital. The nurse is going to give you something for pain, so just lay back and try to relax." His voice sounds far away, so I assume the medicine he mentioned is already working its way into my system, making him sound muffled.

I don't know how long I lay there, seeing as the wondrous liquid being piped into my veins must have knocked me out, but I'm woken by the gentle voice of the doctor. "Ok… let's get this scan so I can get you stitched or rather stapled up. You've been here long enough… sorry about that. The ER got rather busy."

"How long was I asleep?" I blink the cobweb feeling from my eyes and scan the room.

"About three hours now." The sensation of cool liquid coats my side, and I wince when he presses the wand against my skin. "This will be quick." He moves it around, staring at the tiny screen that looks like an eighty's tv going bad. "Alright. Doesn't look like you damaged anything, so I'm going to irrigate this again and then get you stapled up." He wipes me off and then gathers some supplies. The nurse hands him a bottle of something, which he unceremoniously squirts into the hole.

"Fuck…" I groan as the pain skitters across my skin. "Thought you said the pain meds would make this *not* hurt." I bite down on my lip and puff out a pained breath.

He wipes me down. "Sorry, sweetheart. That was unavoidable. You may feel a slight burn. I'm going to numb the area, so the staples don't hurt you." The doctor keeps working and I watch through hazy eyes as he grabs what looks like a run-of-the-mill staple gun. "Ok Mrs. Gresham, you're going to feel some pulling as I put these in."

I hide my reaction to him calling me Mrs. Gresham, assuming Hunter lied and said we were married. "Can my husband come back here?" I'm not sure if I should be mad or relieved, but before I can think about it too much, the doctor is covering the stapled area with gauze.

"I'll send someone to fetch him. With the business in the ER, we didn't have time to get him in here. In the meantime, I'm going to write you a script for antibiotics and get your discharge papers together. A nurse will be in to explain how to care for the injury. I'd suggest start by not carrying any glass around wet pavement."

He walks out, leaving me to stare at the ceiling. So far, so good at not running into any complications. I just wish Hunter was back here—honestly, I wish it was Gage, but I know why he had to stay back.

"Honey, are you in danger?" A nurse who looks to be close in age to me presses her hand to my shoulder, making me flinch.

"What?" I blink my confusion away and furrow my brows. "No... I told you I fell."

"Okay, sweetheart. You just rest. I'll take care of you—you're safe here."

"I told you—I'm not in danger." She walks out without giving my words any thought and I shift nervously on the hospital bed. The last thing we need is for some nosey nurse thinking I'm in trouble.

It feels like forever before someone comes back to my room, but the moment the nurse from earlier steps into the tiny space, I know something is off. "Um... can you get my husband?"

The nurse moves around the room without saying anything to me, making the hairs stand up on the back of my neck. "Hey—I asked if you could get my husband."

She finally stops moving and turns to me. "Sweetheart, I don't think he's coming. He left."

"Left?" I push myself up, gritting my teeth through the pain. "No. That can't be right. He wouldn't leave me. Please go out and check again." Panic burrows its way into my chest. I know there is no way Hunter would leave me here. She must be mistaken. I lean my head back and close my eyes, praying like hell this is some kind of nightmare, but then I realize my nightmare is real—and in the form of my *stepbrother*.

"Don't worry, Poppy. I got here as *soon* as I could."

19

———

Gage

It's been over three fucking hours and we haven't heard a word out of Hunter—or Poppy, for that matter. I'm sure my incessant pacing is driving Danny crazy, but I can't help but think something has happened. Why else wouldn't they have called?

"Please stop pacing." Danny waves his hand at me. "I called Perez. He's heading over to the hospital to check things out. It's not uncommon for an ER to take this long. Just relax... Perez will call us once he's there."

"He should have sent someone over when we called earlier. Why didn't he?"

Danny shakes his head at me. "You know why. He didn't want to draw too much attention to them. The last thing we need is for someone to find out you're here. Alessandro would be on us like flies on shit."

I know he's right, but it doesn't lessen the rage I feel. All I can think about is *her* being there without me. These are feelings I'm unfamiliar with and it's disconcerting, to say the

154

least. I've not allowed myself to feel attachments like this to anyone other than my brothers. Thinking about them makes my chest tighten with unease. I haven't talked to them in almost a month—which is by far the longest we've ever gone without speaking.

Danny is watching me as I sit down. "Any chance you can check on my brother, Drake? I hate not being able to call him. Maybe he can give you an update or something."

His expression softens. "I can call Archer... I probably already should have. He needs to know what happened."

I watch as he tugs his phone out and sets it on the table in front of him. He swipes the screen awake and taps something. Ringing fills the room and I realize he's calling Archer on speaker. "Downs." His gruff voice fills the line as Danny leans forward to speak.

"Archer, we have a problem." Danny flicks his gaze at me. "Poppy got injured and Hunter had to take her to the ER. They've been there for 3 plus hours with no word. Perez is heading over there, but I wanted to bring you up to speed."

Danny cuts right to the chase, telling me what I thought all along. He's just as worried as I am. "Fuck. What happened?" Archer's aggravated tone grates through the tiny device speaker.

"She slipped and fell, landing belly side down on the glass she was holding. It shattered and impaled her. Gage was able to remove the embedded piece, but it was bad. Hunter took her in to be evaluated."

"Okay. It's not unusual for it to take several hours at most hospitals."

Dany clicks his tongue. "True... but Hunter isn't answering texts or calls. Is that like *him*? Would he ignore us while guarding a client?"

"Well, *no*. Perez trains his guys the same way I do. Have you heard from Perez yet?" I can't stop the anxious feeling bubbling inside me as I listen to them talk.

Danny does something to his phone, then sets it back down. "No. I just sent him a text asking him for a status update. I fucked up Archer. I should've insisted Perez sent another man with them."

"You did the right thing, Danny. The more people with them, the more suspicious it would look. Let me make some calls." The line goes dead, and I watch as Danny covers his face with his hands.

He's beating himself up over this situation, even though we don't know anything is wrong. "You did what you were supposed to do." I blow out a breath. "I'm sure you're right, and Hunter is just preoccupied. I, of all people, know how an ER can get. Hell... maybe he doesn't have service inside. You and I both know he isn't going to leave her side."

He nods. "Yeah... I hope you're right." Danny stands and pockets his phone. "I'm going to walk the perimeter. I need to clear my head until we hear back."

"Fine. I'll finish cleaning up the kitchen." I cleaned up most of the mess, but there was still some dried blood on the hardwood floors.

Needing a distraction, I pull out some spray and grab paper towels. I don't want Poppy to come home and see the mess because it will only make her feel guilty. Kneeling down on the hard surface, I spritz the cleaner over the droplets of maroon leading from the backdoor. Her blood pools with the liquid, turning it a gross brown color. Taking care to get every last smudge up, I inch my way to the door and stare out toward the pool. The whole back deck of concrete is tinged red.

Muttering some profanities to myself, I push outside and search for a hose. It looks like we slaughtered a pig back here, which makes me shudder because the reality is—that's Poppy's blood. I'm not squeamish, but seeing *her* blood covering the cement like paint, my stomach rolls with a putrid feeling. I've never been bothered by the sight of gruesome things. Hell, I've seen bones protruding from people's flesh, but this—this makes me want to vomit.

Staring down at the stained ground, my mind immediately conjures up the past and I'm suddenly taken back to that night that changed everything.

I move toward my mother's still form. "I know, buddy. I know. But mom needs help, so go call 9-1-1." I watch as he makes the call. I faintly hear the operator's voice in the background, but all I can focus on is my mother.

Rolling her to her back carefully, I press my head against her chest. Not hearing any sounds to make me think she's breathing, I tilt her head back, worried I'm doing more damage than good. "Please mom… you have to be okay." I blow a breath into her mouth, willing the air into her lungs.

"One, two, three…" I count the beats as I press her chest. It feels like hours before someone is tapping my shoulder.

Snapped from the moment, I find that Danny is actually tapping me. My eyes take a moment to focus. "Hey man, you okay?" He gives me a look that reeks of concern. "I've been calling your name for a few minutes."

"Yeah—sorry. I was lost in thought." I glance at the blood-stained ground one more time and shrug. "I figured I should get this cleaned up." That's when I notice Danny's expression has changed—and it's one that sends unadulterated fear through my veins. "What is it?"

He takes a breath. "Perez is at the hospital. We need to go, Gage."

"Why, Danny—why do we need to go?" I clench my fingers into fists at my sides. "You said it would be too dangerous for us both to be there."

Danny palms the back of his neck. "They're gone."

"What do you mean, they're *gone*?" I spit my words. "It's a fucking hospital. Patients don't just up and disappear without help or by *force*. And where in the fuck is Hunter? He wouldn't just take her without telling you, would he?"

"No—fuck." Danny closes his eyes. "I don't know. He's not one of ours, Gage. But Perez swears his guy wouldn't do anything like this. He's interviewing the staff now. Let's go so we can help him figure out what the hell is going on. Archer is on his way, too. He'll be here in a couple of hours."

I scoff at his words. In a couple of hours, she could be *dead* if she's been taken. "Whatever. Let's just get to the hospital. You better hope this guy, *Hunter,* isn't the reason Poppy is gone."

I storm past him and into the house. Stomping up the steps, I quickly change my shirt and slip on my shoes. When my eyes catch the black duffle bag, my mind blanks out. I know I swore I'd never touch another gun again, but Poppy might be in danger. Not giving myself time to chicken out, I slip the pistol from inside and shove it in the waistband at my back. I rush downstairs to find Danny and get moving. But the need to punch something or someone is bristling at the surface, and I slam my fist into the sheetrock beside the front door. Pain radiates up my arm and I clutch my fingers against my chest.

"Chill out, Gage. The last thing we need is you hurt, too. I get it. You're pissed off." Danny rounds the front of the car. "I am too. This shouldn't have happened."

Not wanting to hear a damn word he's saying, I climb into the SUV and slam the door. My mind is swirling with every possible scenario as Danny slowly turns around the car. He doesn't say anything as he pulls onto the two-lane road.

"How far is the hospital?" I grumble as I stare out into the wooded landscape.

"About thirty minutes."

With the lack of traffic on the road, we pull into the emergency room parking lot a lot faster than anticipated. Danny spots Perez standing outside the entrance. "There's Perez."

I'm out of the car before it comes to a complete stop and march my ass toward him. Perez holds his hands out, expecting me to throw a punch.

"Whoa... calm down Gage." He steps back as I skitter to a halt in front of him.

"Where the *fuck* is she?" I ball my fists to refrain from taking a swing.

"I don't know. I'm waiting for a hospital administrator to get here. They refuse to give me any information other than she just up and left."

I pace the emergency bay like a caged animal, ready to pounce. "Up and left? Where in the hell is Hunter, then? Huh? Poppy wouldn't just leave without him going with her —or at minimum, he'd be answering his god-damned phone."

Before he can reply, an older man steps through the sliding glass doors. Despite wearing scrubs, I know that this is the administrator we've been waiting for. When he gets closer, I realize I recognize him. And it's mutual. "Gage Winston— never thought I'd see *you* again. And certainly not in Lexington Alabama."

Perez looks between us with a questioning look. "Perez, this is Oscar Hannity. We know each other from medical school."

"Small world—Dr. Hannity, did they explain why we asked to see someone in charge?" Perez cuts right to the chase.

"Yes… something about a patient you believe is in danger or something." He glances back at me. "This one of your patients?"

"No. My girlfriend. Look—" I take a deep breath. "—it's a long story that I'd rather not tell here. Is there somewhere we can talk more privately?" I motion to the two men standing beside me. "This is Jose Perez and Danny Truett. They're my personal security team."

Hannity's eyebrows rise at the mention of personal security. "I knew you'd become some kind of hotshot doctor, but you're famous enough for a security detail?"

"Not exactly. They've been tasked with keeping me and my girlfriend safe. Let's get inside and I'll start from the beginning." Hannity shook his head and starts toward the door.

Knowing Hannity and I go way back, I feel a glimmer of hope that he'll give us what we need without all the red tape. Because the longer it takes to get the details we need, the longer it will take to bring my girl home.

20

Poppy

I STARE at the cold eyes of my stepbrother as he steps into the room.

"How did you get here?" My eyes shift around nervously, willing the nurse to realize something is wrong.

"The lovely nurse from earlier called me as soon as you arrived in the ER. She recognized you from a missing persons flyer I had drawn up and distributed throughout the Southeast." He steps to the foot of the bed and turns toward the nurse that just stepped back inside. "Be a dear and get those papers. I'd like to take Poppy home as soon as possible."

"Of course. I'll just need to make a call." Alessandro watches as the older woman slips out of my room before moving beside me.

"Get up. We're leaving." He jerks my arm, making me cry out from the sudden pain in my side.

"That bitch is probably calling the local cops. You better move faster if you don't want your friend to die."

I suck in a breath. "Hunter?" The IV is suddenly jerked from my arm as Alessandro pulls me to my feet. "Where is he?"

"Don't you worry about that, Poppy. He's right where I need him to be." The hospital gown I was changed into at some point gapes open at the back. I try to hold it closed as he latches onto my upper arm and drags me into the narrow hallway. Ensuring its clear, he pulls toward an emergency exit. "You best not draw any attention to us—or I'll put a bullet in your head. Got me?"

I nod as hot tears stream down my face. The bright sun makes me squint as my feet scuff against the blacktop while he drags me toward a waiting car. As we get closer, I see Eduardo leaning against the passenger door. His lecherous gaze makes me shudder in disgust and the fear of death is suddenly replaced with something worse—fear of him raping me. Eduardo yanks open the back door and I'm thrown inside. I whimper when I halfway land on Hunter's unconscious frame. His hands are zip tied together, and he's been gagged. There's a slight trickle of blood oozing from a gash on his forehead, but he at least appears to be breathing.

"What the fuck did you do?" I growl, reaching out to touch him, but the sudden force of Alessandro's backhand sends me into the door.

His seedy eyes bore into me as he grips my hair in his fist. "You will not talk to me like that. You've caused me nothing but trouble, Poppy. As far as your friend—" he jerks his head in Hunter's direction. "I haven't done anything, *yet*. That will be up to you…"

I lean back against the seat, my fingers tugging Hunters into mine. It's my fault he's laying here looking like death, yet all I can think about is Gage. He's going to lose his shit when he realizes we're gone. God, I want to strangle that nurse… if she'd only minded her own fucking business.

We drive for about fifteen minutes when I see Alessandro pulling the car down a gravel drive. A small metal building is tucked back off the road, making this the perfect place to kill me. I stifle a cry, not wanting to fuel either of their anger. When Eduardo climbs out the front, he rips open my door and jerks me out by my ankles. I clutch at my side, not surprised to find my gown wet with blood. My yelp of pain as my ass hits the ground doesn't faze him. In fact, I swear it eggs him on, making him tug harder. I try clawing at the ground to stop my forward movement, but the only thing I accomplish is ripping the skin from my fingertips. Fortunately, the trek across the rocky surface is short, and I'm hauled into a chair. My stomach is soaking wet from the reopened injury, dying the blue and white hospital gown crimson.

Eduardo yanks my hands behind me and fastens my arms to the back of the chair. The plastic binds he uses cut into my skin and I hiss at the pain.

"Why are you doing this? Can't you just let me go?" I plead, knowing it won't get me anywhere with him.

Eduardo moves around to my front and grips my jaw in his fingers. The force of his grip will surely leave marks behind, but I hold my breath, refusing to show him it hurts. "The only way you'll leave is in a body bag, puta." He shoves my head away and stalks toward the door, where Alessandro is dragging Hunter.

I watch as they dump his listless body on the ground and kick him for good measure. "He was so easy to overpower. I paid one of the cute nurses to tell him your boyfriend was outside, and he bought it—hook, line and sinker. Eduardo here jabbed him with the sedative and the rest... well—you'll see."

"Please..." I whimper, my eyes filling with tears again. "Just let him go—you have me, that's all you need."

Alessandro grabs him by the hair, jerking Hunter's head upright. "No. This motherfucker isn't the one I want, Poppy. I want that coward who stole you from me. This piece of skin is only good for drawing him out." Eduardo returns carrying a bucket and I watch in horror as he dumps it over Hunter's body.

He jerks awake, his eyes looking around wildly when his gaze lands on me. "Poppy."

"Shut up, gringo." Alessandro presses a gun to Hunter's head, and he stills. "Now... you two are going to tell me what I want to know, or I'll put a bullet in your heads. I'll start with you."

Eduardo grips Hunter by the arms and lifts him to his feet. He manhandles him over to the wall, where his hands are strung up on some kind of hook. Alessandro tucks the gun into his waistband and bends down to grab something from the ground. When he lifts it up, I gasp.

"No... Alessandro, please don't do this." He flips the wooden handle in his hand, his wicked grin sending ice through my veins as he glances over his shoulder at me.

The sickle in his hand is rusted, but even from here I can tell it's still deadly. "So... Hunter—" Alessandro laughs in a twisted way, almost sounding like Hannibal Lecter, as he moves closer to where Hunter hangs. "How about we make this simple and you tell me where your buddy Gage is hiding?"

"Fuck you." Hunter spits at Alessandro's feet. "You obviously don't know who the hell you're dealing with."

I want to scream at him—tell him that he's the one who doesn't know, but words fail me as I watch Alessandro swing the metal edge, connecting it with Hunter's abdomen. Hunter cries out, unable to stop his reaction from the blade slicing across his skin. As if it's not enough, I watch my demented step-brother make three more swings with the blade, splitting open Hunter's skin like a hotdog you've cooked too long in the microwave. Once he's good and bloody, Eduardo jerks him from his perch on the wall and shoves him to the ground on his knees. Hunter is barely conscious, but I can see the fight in his eyes. He looks like a man who is willing to die for me, and that makes my breath stutter.

"Hunter." I half sob as I call his name. "*Please* Alessandro... stop this."

"You ready to give up the doctor?" He moves behind Hunter and wraps his arm around his neck. "Tell me, Poppy. Whose life is more important—the man who failed to protect you?" Hunter's face reddens as he tightens his grip. "Or the man who failed to keep his promises to *always* be there?"

I can't control the sob that bubbles up and breaks free. "This isn't right... please. I'll go home with you. I'll—" I suck in a shuddering breath. "I'll marry Eduardo... whatever you want —just don't do this, *please* Alessandro..." I'm full-on begging him to stop this madness.

He releases Hunter's throat and rushes toward me. His hand shoots out and grips my throat as he brings my face inches from his. "Eduardo doesn't want your tainted pussy, Poppy. You're useless to me now… no—that's a lie. I'm going to break you in ways you can't imagine, and I'm going to do it as your doctor watches. Then… when while you think you can't take anymore, I'm going to kill him and let you watch the life drain from his eyes before I snuff you from existence."

I hiccup a sob as he releases his hold. The palm of his hand connects with my cheek before he moves back to Hunter—who is barely hanging on. Eduardo jerks him to his knees as Alessandro calls my name.

"Poppy… I asked you a question. Where. Is. the. Doctor?"

My gaze holds his callus eyes a moment before panning to Eduardo. I know in my heart nothing I say is going to matter. We're going to die, anyway. I slowly lower my gaze to Hunter, who is watching me with a look that makes my heart stop.

"*Please.*" I beg Alessandro, hoping he'll hear me, knowing he won't.

He pulls his gun from his waistband and presses the barrel against Hunter's head. "I'll ask you one more time, Poppy. Otherwise, the first bullet has *his* name on it."

I whimper, my eyes landing on Hunter's gaze again. He gives me a slight shake of his head, a silent order not to tell him what he wants. I watch as he mouths '*it's okay*' as the hot tears sting my eyes.

"Hunter…" I whisper his name, knowing what comes next. "I'm so sorry…" My head jerks towards Alessandro. "Don't do this."

"You fucked with the wrong man, Poppy."

The echo of the gun firing bounces off the walls like a glass shattering. I watch in horror as Hunter's body falls to the side, his lifeless eyes staring at me from the pool of blood his face rests in. I don't even hear my own screams as I'm suddenly jerked from the chair. My hands burn from the plastic ties, cutting into my wrists before snapping off the wooden slats of my seat. I can't tear my eyes off Hunter's still body, my heart threatening to beat out of my chest from the fear and anguish I'm feeling.

I knew Alessandro was a monster—but *this*?

He killed a man in cold blood all because I wanted a life free of him... only to be trapped in a prison far worse than Hell.

21

Gage

AFTER EXPLAINING EVERYTHING TO HANNITY, he's more than willing to help. He gives Danny access to the security footage while Perez and I speak with some of the staff. It doesn't take long to figure out what happened. Apparently, Alessandro posted several missing persons flyers back home. As serendipitous as it was, the nurse currently sobbing her eyes out saw the flyer while visiting her daughter a week ago. She recognized Poppy and called her daughter—who called the hotline on the flyer.

Danny steps into the tiny room we're all standing in, talking to the nurse with a forlorn expression. "Let me guess— Alessandro was here?" I fold my arms across my chest.

"Yeah. And it gets worse." He looks over at Perez, who visibly stiffens. "He has Hunter too. It's clear as damn day on the footage. Eduardo sticks Hunter in the neck with something and he goes down like a sack of potatoes."

"Fuck." Perez scrubs his face with his palm. "I need to make a call."

I watch as he steps from the room and turns back to Danny. "How did this happen?" he asks, moving into the room more.

The nurse babbles through her sobs. "I'm so sorry... I thought she was in danger... I... I—" She turns and runs from the room, leaving Hannity and Danny stunned.

"This is a big fucking mess." Hannity blows out a breath. "I need to contact the authorities. You understand that, right?" He looks between us. "A patient was kidnapped from my hospital—this is going to send the board into a tizzy."

I nod in understanding. "Danny—how far out is Archer?"

"I'm here." Archer's voice cuts through the space like an angel's choir. "Perez filled me in a little. His team is en route to help us. We're going back to the safe house to strategize."

Filing out of the hospital room, Archer gives Hannity his contact information, telling him to have the police call him. For now, we need to figure out what happens next. All we know is that Alessandro has them both—which won't end well.

The ride back to the safe house is silent. Archer spends his time on the phone, and Danny is eerily silent. I know he blames himself, but Perez and Archer have repeatedly told him he followed protocol. But when your charge goes missing, along with one of your colleagues, you can't help fault yourself.

I'm surprised to see a ton of vehicles in the driveway. "What's going on?"

"Perez and his team are here. We're going to find them and bring them home."

Climbing from the car, I'm suddenly overwhelmed with emotions and I falter in my steps. Danny grabs my arm to steady me. "Hey man… you good?"

I shake my head, because honestly, I'm not. "No. The time I need my family, I can't call them. But it's fine. The sooner we find her and bring her home, the better."

As we step inside, I'm taken aback by the number of people standing inside. A massive man stands off to the side, chatting with a beautiful brunette. At the table is another man and woman who seem to be completely engrossed with something on the screen of the laptop they're staring at. Perez sees us and waves us inside.

"Let me introduce you to my team."

"Guys, you know Archer–this is Danny Truett, one of Archer's guys. And this is Gage Winston." Four sets of eyes land on me. "Gage, this is my team—Maddy and Noah are actually my partners in the company. And those two, Byron Danvil and Allison Smiley, served with Maddy before she retired from the Navy. Now they work for us."

The name registers, and I turn my gaze to hers. "I'm sorry, Miss Smiley."

She forces a smile. "Hunter is tough—I know he will do whatever needs to be done to bring her home."

I swallow the bile, praying to God she's right. But this isn't the desert, and this enemy is even more vile than the ones he's used to from his time in the sandbox. I don't say it though, I can't. Knowing her fiancé may not come back eats at my core, because it was my decision to take Poppy out of the ER instead of doing it the right way.

I listen as they the hash a plan, even if it makes no sense to me. We still have no idea where he's gotten off to with either of them. And glancing at the clock, it's been almost six hours since I put her in the car with Hunter and told her I loved her.

Archer's phone interrupts the chattering of voices and I watch as he stands with the device pressed to his ear. His body is rigid as he moves out of the kitchen and into the living room.

"No. I don't give a fuck about that, Alex." Archer cuts his eyes toward me, and I know whatever it is, it's not good news. "Get your ass in a car and get here. I'll text you the location—and for fuck's sake, don't tell Drake. He has enough on his plate right now."

Archer shoves the phone in his pocket and blows out a frustrated breath. "What is it?"

"Let's go in the kitchen. This is going to change things—and Gage." Archer pauses. "Remember, this is Alessandro's doing. Not yours... not Poppy's."

Fuck. Now I know that whatever that phone call was, I'm not going to like it. I amble in behind him and lean against the wall. Maddy, Noah, and Perez are leaned against the counter, mumbling about something. Allison and Byron are still busy working the traffic cameras, the few that there are, in hopes of seeing something out of the norm.

"Can I have everyone's attention—actually? Perez, can we chat first, privately?"

He nods and I watch as they head outside onto the back deck. I see Archer's mouth move and Perez's body goes ramrod straight. His gaze glances our way, settling on Allison and I know, without a doubt, the news has something to do with Hunter.

Archer and Perez step back inside, and Perez immediately goes to Noah and whispers something into his ear. Noah's eyes widen and he nods, his eyes landing on their friend and co-worker. Perez gives Archer a silent twitch of his head, telling him to go ahead with the information.

"First—Alex Whitmire will be joining us in about two hours."

"Why is my brother's criminal defense attorney coming here?" All heads swivel to look in my direction.

Archer clears his throat. "Alex intercepted a message intended for Drake thirty minutes ago. The package has information in it regarding Poppy and Hunter."

"What kind of information?" Allison pipes up, just as eager as me to find out anything about the two of them.

Perez presses his hand against her shoulder. "We'll wait for him to get here to go into detail."

"No." She pushes back her seat and stands. "If you know something, we—" she waves her hand at me. "Deserve to know. Don't try to coddle me, Jose—or I'll kick you in your fucking prosthetic." Allison balls her fists at her side, her breaths bordering on that of a raging bull ready to charge.

Noah steps forward. "Sit down, Allison." He all but shoves her into the chair as Maddy kneels between her and Byron.

"Allison," her tone is a dead giveaway that something bad is about to come out, and I take a step forward. "Sweetheart— the package has evidence proving he took Hunter and Poppy. Though we already know that from the security footage."

"What aren't you telling me?" She looks at her friend and I can see the heartbreak in Maddy's eyes as she looks back at Noah for guidance.

Maddy tugs Allison's hands into hers and sighs. "Hunter's gone, Ally. Alessandro killed him."

The blood rushes to my ears and all I can hear is the sound of it pumping through my veins. I vaguely hear her scream something before she runs past me and the sound of the front door slamming snaps me back to the present.

"Poppy." My voice cracks with emotion as I voice the only name that matters right now. And maybe that's horrendous of me, but I need to know if she's gone, too.

Archer snaps his gaze to meet my panicked expression. "We don't know. The information only showed what he'd done to Hunter. But regardless, Gage. It's a warning. He's a sick mother fucker and if Poppy comes out of this alive, it'll be a miracle. Either way, she's not going to escape unscathed. If she survives, there's going to be damage, and some of it may be irreparable."

"What was in the box?" I ask, my body moving forward on it its own until I collapse in a vacant chair. "Archer?" I turn to pin him with a glare. "What was *in* the box?"

He looks over his shoulder… I assume, to make sure Allison isn't inside. "Photos of his body and a token of proof."

"Token of proof?" I narrow my eyes at him, not under-standing.

I finally notice Danny, who is looking worse for the wear. He pulls the chair opposite me and sits down. "It's bad, isn't it?"

Archer nods. "Aside from the pictures Alex described, he said Hunter's dog tags were included." He closes his eyes and swallows. "And they were wrapped in what appeared to be human flesh."

"What the fuck? Human flesh? How can Alex be sure?"

Archer glances toward the front door again. "Because it was tattooed skin, Gage. And after talking with Perez, he confirmed the tattoo was Hunter's."

I scramble from my seat, barely making it to the sink before losing the contents of my stomach. As a doctor, gruesome is second nature, but hearing that a man tasked with protecting the woman I love was butchered like that makes me sick. I turn the water on and cup my hands beneath the stream, desperate to wash the vile taste from my mouth.

"He was supposed to be married in two months." I hang my head down, shame burning through my veins at the carnage one decision has created.

"This isn't your fault."

"Isn't it?" I push up and turn to face him. "If I'd only taken her to Drake and let him stash her using Angels Wings like we've done thousands of times before—that woman out there wouldn't be feeling gut wrenching loss."

Danny pushes to his feet. "Well, if I would've sent someone with them, they would still be here. Lots of shoulda, coulda, wouldas here, Gage." He glares at me, daring me to argue.

"Bullshit." I snap. "This is not your doing, Danny. As much as I want to take blame, deep down I know the responsibility is on one person and one person alone. Alessandro Hugo. And if I have anything to say about what happens next, I want him dead."

"How about you don't go making those threats out loud? I'd like to be able to defend you honestly when the time comes." Alex's voice interrupts our conversations and Archer turns to greet him.

"Let me see it." He holds out his hands, taking the box that Alex thrusts toward him.

Alex gives me a half-hearted smile. "You and your brother sure know how to pick 'em."

"What the fuck does *that* mean?" I level him with a look that makes him throw his hands up in defense.

He shrugs his shoulders. "Oh, I forgot—you've been off the radar. Let's just say you're not the only brother who's fallen prey to a woman. And from what I understand, they're *both* tied to Alessandro Hugo as well."

My expression does little to hide the surprise. "Explain… now."

Alex spends the next twenty minutes filling us in on Drake's woman and how her husband tried to kill her. Apparently, he was working for Alessandro Hugo, which is how Eduardo got out so fast. But that's not what brought them together. She sought him out after her husband, the *Judge*, nearly killed her. And according to Archer—he nearly did, anyway. Alex explained that Drake was currently at home with Rhiannon while she recuperated from being hanged and left for dead. The Judge had used his power to falsify a warrant and had her arrested. When she was brought in, he took her and tortured her.

He's apparently as sick as Alessandro. I can see why they'd partner up. It pains me not to be home for my sibling, knowing the woman he's fallen in love with could use my expertise—but Archer assures me he's fine.

"How's Roland?" I look over at Archer, who smiles. "Please tell me he isn't involved in anything as shitty as Drake or me."

"I can't answer that… but I will say this." Archer laughs despite our current situation. "He's chasing a woman, too."

"Fuck." I shake my head. "I hope she isn't as much work as ours have been."

"I have no idea. At least, to my knowledge, *she* has no ties to Alessandro Hugo, so that's a plus," he says honestly. "Ok… let's talk about what happens next."

"I'll tell you what happens next." All four of us swing our gaze to Allison, who is standing in the doorway. "I'm going to find those two motherfuckers and kill them."

"Whoa there, doll." Alex stands up from the table. "Let's not go making threats. Like I told him—" he hooks his thumb over his shoulder at me. "I need to be able to honestly say my clients are innocent."

She narrows her red-rimmed eyes on him. "Well, good thing I'm not your client and I don't give a fuck about being innocent."

Allison spins on her heel and storms out, leaving us all slack-jawed. "Is someone going to go after her?"

Alex looks around the room and when none of make a motion to move, he grumbles, "Really? No? Fine, I'll go after her. We can't be going all half-cocked. It makes my job a lot harder."

Once he leaves the room, Perez clears his throat. "Based on the photos, I think I know where she is—or at least was."

"Well... what in the fuck are we waiting for?" I stand up. "Let's go find Poppy and bring her home."

Archer presses my shoulder. "Slow down, cowboy. We need a plan."

22

Poppy

I HAVE no idea how long I've been forced to sit here and stare at the man whose life I helped end. At this point, rigor mortis has started to set in, and the smell permeating the room is rancid at best. I'm doing everything I can to keep the bile down that threatens to burst out of me like a volcano exploding. Night has fallen, so at least now all I can actually *see* is the outline of Hunter's lifeless corpse in the faint light seeping in from the full moon outside.

My mind continues to replay the moment the gun fired, and I see his beautiful eyes staring at me with terrified realization as his head burst open. As if that wasn't enough emotional damage, I watched in complete horror as they carved out a chunk of his flesh. His hollow stare is burned into my retinas, leaving a permanent scar that can never be erased. I don't deserve to forget it, anyway. Because of me, a woman will bury the man she loved—a man she's expecting to *marry* in sixty days. A sob ruptures from my chest, the sound more like a dying bird since I've cried my throat raw and have no tears left in my body. Periodically, Eduardo comes in to check on me—as if I have anywhere to go. The motherfucker has me strapped to the thin metal wall like a dog.

I'm pretty sure my staples have popped out. Maybe not all of them, but enough that I bled continuously until a little bit ago. My hospital gown is a putrid shade of brown, a combination of blood and dirt. The pain ripples through my system in waves, but I've grown used to it. Hell, it's the only thing reminding me I'm not dead yet. And as much as I'd welcome death right now, all I have to do is glance in front of me to know I can't give up... or Hunter's death will be for nothing.

The sound of the metal door banging open makes me jump. "You ready to tell us what we want to know, puta?"

I lift my head enough to look at the monster standing before me and somehow manage to conjure enough saliva in my mouth to spit at his feet. "Fuck you, Alessandro." My throat burns with every word I speak. "I'll die by your hands sooner rather than later—I won't give up the only man who ever loved me."

The blow to my face isn't surprising. I've endured hundreds over the last couple of years, so today's is nothing new. His fingers dig into my hair as he grabs a fistful and yanks, making my eyes water from the sting. If I have any left when this is said and done, it'll be a miracle. Alessandro bends down, putting his face inches from mine. Even in the dim light, I can see the rage behind his eyes.

"You won't have to. He'll show himself. Before long, they'll know about your little friend and his... *untimely* demise. The package I sent his brother will have arrived by now. Imagine their surprise when they find your bodyguard's dog tags wrapped in his skin. Think that will send them the message they fucked with the wrong man? See, Poppy," His breath makes my insides twist with disgust. "When someone takes something that belongs to me, I make sure they learn a lesson." His fingers trail my neck before tightening around my throat. "You made a mistake running away—but an even bigger one when you opened your legs for that man. So no… you won't die sooner rather than later, because I'm not *finished* with you yet."

He releases my neck and I gag. "I don't know what my mother saw in your father—did she know she married into a family of monsters?"

Alessandro's sinister laugh makes my skin crawl. "I'm sure she realized it the day I killed her, Poppy."

I suck in a breath at his words. "My mom died in a car accident—"

He cuts me off with the tisk of his tongue. "Tsk, tsk, tsk, Poppy. So naive for a woman your age. Sure… her car went off the road, but that was after I tortured her and shoved her body into the driver's seat. Do you know how hard it was to push that car off the road like that?"

"*Why?*" I half-cry, half-sob.

"Power, of course. It's *always* about power. My father was pussy-whipped by your mother. Can't say I blame him entirely, but he had *no* right to make provisional changes to his will. He left her *everything* and me nothing—not as long as she walked this Earth, anyway. I should have known killing him wouldn't be enough to inherit the keys of the kingdom."

I close my eyes and try to calm myself. This man is a complete lunatic. He killed his own father, then my mother— for what? Power? Money? There is no doubt in my mind the only life he values is his own. And despite wanting to live for the sacrifice Hunter made, I send a silent plea for death to take me. That's the endgame here, and I can't—no, *won't*—give him the satisfaction of torturing anyone else I love.

"You're *sick*." I hiss at him, determined to push him hard enough that he slips up and ends my life. It's the only way to protect the only person left I care about. "You're nothing but a scared little boy who can't earn power without intimidation. What does that say about you? I'll tell you what it says —" I lean forward from my uncomfortable perch on the ground, my head tilts up to look him in the face. "It says you're a pussy."

His foot shoots out, the heal of his pristine dress shoe catching me on the side of my head. Pain is instant as my vision swims with darkness and my head snaps to the side. I don't fight back or even attempt to lift my face again... I don't have the energy. Instead, with every blow he delivers, I think of Gage. His image is the only thing I can cling to as my consciousness fades to darkness.

Unfortunately, that lasts two point three seconds because ice cold water rains down on me and I gasp for air. This time, when my eyes open, the light inside the metal prison is on and I have to blink to adjust my eyesight. Even still, my vision is blurry, most likely from the blows to my face and the blood dripping down from my forehead. Eduardo removes my binds from the wall and drags me to where Hunter's body lays. He tosses me against his stiff frame and leans down. The smell is overwhelming, and I start dry-heaving.

"Better get used to that stench... he's going to keep you warm until we figure out where your coward boyfriend is hiding."

Eduardo tugs my arm out and loops the plastic bind around my wrist, then around Hunter's. His skin is cool to the touch and hard. I turn my head and retch bile onto the floor. It's mostly stomach acid which burns the inside of my throat as it comes out. Closing my eyes, I press my free hand down on the cement only to have it land in something wet. Jerking it back like I touched the burner on a stove, I close my fist. The substance is sticky with what feels like shards of glass mixed in. Stupidly, I turn my head and open my eyes to look. This time my stomach revolts and the bile comes out without warning when I see what I've touched.

Eduardo laughs. "Guess you didn't like him for his brains."

Squeezing my lids shut again, I tune out the sounds and focus on the rushing of blood in my ears. My heart beats like a stampede of horses inside my chest and I home in on the sound, counting the thumps in my head. *One... two... three... four.* I can't stop the cadence in my mind—it's the only way to keep from going completely insane.

"Close your eyes all you want, Poppy." Alessandro calls out from somewhere in the room, but I refuse to look. Instead, I hold on to the mantra of my pulse thundering inside me, so I don't acknowledge the man I'm tied against. "The end will be the same."

The metal door clangs so loud, the ringing in my ears is a welcome pain, because it, too, helps drown out the outside world. Even if I survive this, will I be the same?

Because this is what nightmares are made of... and *nightmares* never go away completely.

23

Gage

THE LOCAL POLICE got wind of what's happening and notified the FBI, and our window of time is decreasing. At least, it has if we want to do this without them involved. Alex is losing his shit because he knows we aren't going to wait. Archer has called in two additional guys from his team to assist.

"Here's the deal. What we're about to do is not completely legal because local law enforcement all but ordered us sit tight while they can gather needed warrants and a team to meet us. That's gonna take two hours." He glances around the room at the faces, listening intently. "Poppy may not have two hours. Hell… we aren't even sure she's still alive." My growl causes him to shoot me a glare. "But I suspect she is— and Hunter was a message. Now, Hunter wasn't one of ours —" he looks at Danny and the two men standing beside him. "But I have no doubt he gave his life for her. *I'm* not going to stand idly by and wait for them to get here so they can fuck this up some more, but I can't force any of you to risk your careers."

Alex grumbles behind me.

"What's your problem?" Allison Smiley shoots daggers at him, her entire body radiating with anger.

He palms his neck and blows out a frustrated breath. "We can just storm in there and kill them. I get you're pissed he killed your co-worker, but this isn't the medieval times—we don't operate on 'eye for an eye' justice."

Allison stalks toward him and I swear you can hear a pin drop as her finger thrusts out and rams him in the sternum. "He didn't *just* kill my co-worker. He killed my fiancé—so excuse me for wanting to see him bleed out like the pig he is. And you know what?" Allison pushes him, causing Alex to take a step back. "I'd spend the rest of my life in prison just to watch the blood drain from his body and the light flicker out of his eyes. He took *everything* from me, and I have no fucks left to give. So you and your goodie-two-shoes, let's-not-storm-the-gates mentality can go climb up the ass of a moose for all I care."

We watch as she storms past him, and it isn't until the door slams closed that Alex speaks. "What the hell? Didn't you assholes think that was an important detail to share? I wouldn't have been so fucking heartless with my words." He shakes his head. "Fuck this... you're going to do whatever you want, anyway. And the less I know, the better. I can't incriminate you on details I'm not privy to," He turns on his heel and exits the same way Allison went moments ago.

"Well, *that* was interesting." Noah Murphy's deep voice echoes through the silent room. "But he's right. We can't forget that Hunter wasn't just a member of this team—he was Allison's life and that's been ripped away from her. She is going to struggle with this, and nothing we can do will change that. Or her gung-ho attitude. But bringing Poppy home can be how we honor his memory. It's what he would have wanted. Gage." He turns to look at me. "You don't know me well enough to know this, but I don't play by the rules." He glances at his watch. "We've got roughly ninety minutes before this place is swarming with Feds. Let's get moving and bring home your girl."

Everyone nods in agreement, and we pile into the cars waiting out front. Archer looks over at me from the front seat of the SUV. We've split up into two vehicles. Archer, Danny and the two new guys who I now know as Brian and Doug are with me. Noah, Maddy, Perez and Allison are in the other. In addition, Noah has a few others meeting us at the location we think Hunter was killed. Archer goes over the plan again, reminding me that I am only in the car because of my medical training. He wants me to be on standby if someone is hurt—but I'm hoping the only ones hurt are Alessandro and Eduardo. Those two won't get an ounce of medical care from me. I might even speed up their reunion in Hell if given the chance. Maddy will remain in the SUV monitoring every-thing with a drone. She's apparently some kind of whiz when it comes to counterintelligence and is best suited behind the scenes. Plus... if I had to bet, she's physically unable to help right now. But I have bigger problems to deal with right now and her medical state isn't one of them.

I notice Perez and the others are pulled off to the side just south of a gravel driveway. Archer swings in behind them and cuts the engine. My heart races as I climb from the car, and I know it's not just because I'm way out of my depth being here—it's because of the heavy gun Danny shoves into my hand.

"I know how you feel, but for today, you have to put that aside."

I don't tell him about the gun I have in my waistband that's been there since the hospital. Instead, I nod in agreement. "I'll do whatever it takes to save her, Danny. Even if that means losing myself all over again."

He grips my shoulder. "Let's hope it doesn't come to that."

"Or let's do." Allison bumps past me and I cringe. She's been destroyed, and I can't assuage the fact it's my fault.

I'm told to stay at the rear of the group, to ensure I don't get shot—seeing as it's likely Alessandro wants to put a bullet in my head. I'll stick behind Archer. This time we're all geared up in bullet-proof vests, so even if he manages to take a shot at one of us, we're slightly protected. My heart is thumping like a raging bull as I hear what Noah is saying through the tiny earpiece wedged in my ear. Behind me is Danny, who gently urges me forward when the all-clear comes through the speaker.

It's rather surprising that there aren't more men lying in wait when we finally make it close enough to assess the building. There are two standing guard at the front door, but aside from them, I don't see anyone else.

"You're going to stay right here." Archer cocks a brow at me, waiting to see if I argue. When I nod my head, he lets out the breath he was holding. "Once we know the scene is secure, I'll signal for you to enter. Do *not*, under any circumstances, come in a moment beforehand. Got it?"

"Yeah. I got it," I grumble, knowing it's smarter for me to be out here than in there. "Just hurry… please."

I stay back, watching as, one by one, they surround the tiny chrome building. Without much fanfare, I witness both guards at the entrance drop to the ground. Allison, Hunter's fiancée, steps around the corner of the building and secures the two men who lay unconscious in the dirt. Noah and Perez drag their inanimate frames toward the wood line, then return to Allison's side.

I'm not prepared mentally or emotionally for what happens next. The three of them enter through the door, and a colossal amount of gunfire and screaming ensues. I can hear shouting in my head, but none of it makes sense. What I *do* make out are the terrifying caterwauls of pain coming from inside. I inch forward, uncertain of what to do. I see Archer and Danny emerge from the rear, hot on the tail of someone. Gunfire erupts as they keep chase, and once again, I freeze. When I hear Perez screaming for Archer or Danny, I don't hesitate.

My feet move on their own and I rush forward, stopping only long enough to peer inside the doorway. As soon as I step through the threshold, my stomach rolls with vomit. Allison is on her knees, crying hysterically beside who I assume is Hunter. Noah is unconscious near the back of the room, his head bleeding profusely. As I pan my eyes toward Allison again, I see Perez on his back, Alessandro over him. Perez is trying to get Allison's attention, but she's lost in her grief.

None of them heard me enter, giving me an advantage. Gripping the gun in my hand, I choke down my nerves and pray I remember how to use it right. Slowly raising the barrel, I squeeze the acrylic grip in an unforgiving hold and pull the trigger. The sound echoes through the room just as the door opens. Spinning my body, Archer holds his hands up in shock.

"Fuck… Gage." He moves forward, grasping the 9mm from me. "Are you hurt?"

Blinking my eyes, it takes me a minute to register his words. "The others," I mutter, turning away from him and moving closer to where Perez was down. He's pushing up from the ground, a very dead Alessandro lying beside him. I start to reach out and aid him, but my eyes connect with the reason for being here.

"*Poppy.*"

My voice breaks at the sight of her. Archer beats me to her side, but we both drop to our knees, checking for signs of life. She appears unconscious, which I'm grateful for, since she's tied to Hunter's dead body like a dog, but I have no idea if she's breathing. Archer pulls a blade from his boot and severs the zip ties digging into her wrists.

"Gage." His voice is filled with concern. "The locals are gonna be swarming this place any second."

"I know." I run my fingers across her throat, feeling for a pulse. "She's got a pulse—a weak one, but it's there." I glance over at the man who gave his life for hers. "I'm sorry about Hunter. Neither of us wanted this to happen—she just wanted to be free."

Archer's eyes pan over to Alessandro. "Well, *he* won't be a problem anymore. Unfortunately, Eduardo got away."

My eyes shoot up to his. "What? How?"

"He got a shot off at us. Danny took one to the shoulder, slowing us down enough to give him the chance." He sighs. "This is an epic fucking mess."

There's a commotion at the door and we glance up to see several men storm in. Maddy is hot on their tail until she sees Allison lying beside Hunter. She runs to Allison's side, dropping to her knees, and pulls her into an embrace. My heart shatters a little more as I watch them crumble over the death of a good man.

"Maddy," Perez calls out, getting her attention. "Noah needs you."

The next several minutes are spent in complete chaos—it's a fucking shitstorm, to say the least. Local law enforcement has this place completely overrun. Between the fire department, coroner and masses of uniforms scouring the grounds, I haven't left Poppy's side. Alessandro's body is taken into custody, as is Hunter's. They're apparently evidence, which isn't taken well by Allison, who was handcuffed after physically attacking one of the patrol officers trying to keep her away from the body bag.

Poppy still hasn't woken up, which isn't surprising considering the massive gash to her head, and based on the crimson stained gown, blood loss exacerbated the problem. The paramedics settle her on the stretcher after getting an IV started and start toward the door. I'm not leaving her side again, so I follow the stretcher toward the front. One of the uniformed officers blocks the doorway, preventing me from stepping out.

"Sir, I'm going to need you to wait a moment." He holds his hand out, blocking the entry.

I push at his forearm, trying to get around. "I need to be with her." As I step around him, I'm surprised when he grips my wrist, twisting my arm behind me. "What the fuck?"

Archer moves toward us, but the officer shakes his head. "I'm sorry, sir, but you're going to have to come with me."

I try to jerk my arm free of him, but he presses me forward, shoving my body into the wall. "I need to go with *her*," I bellow, trying to finagle my way out of his hold. "Why are you doing this? I *need* to be with Poppy."

"I'm sorry, sir, but I have to take you in. You have the right to remain silent. Anything you say can and will be used against you in a court of law. You have the right to an attorney. If you cannot afford an attorney, one will be provided for you. Do you understand your rights?"

"Are you fucking kidding me? You're *arresting* me? The motherfucker I shot kidnapped and brutalized the woman being carted out of here—not to mention murdered a man in cold blood."

Archer steps beside us. "Gage, take a breath. It's standard procedure."

I blink, the reality crashing down on me like a weighted blanket. This is something I'm *very* familiar with, only this is the woman I love, not my mother—and it sickens me that I won't be there when she wakes up. "Yeah... Been here before. Call Alex and... Archer?" I glance at him, knowing I've lost this battle for now. "Call Drake."

24

Poppy

My ENTIRE BODY feels like it has been dragged behind a car across the asphalt. Squeezing my eyes together, I work to pry them apart—fully expecting to see Hunter's dead body when I open them. Instead, my vision is assaulted by a fluorescent glow, and I have to blink through the burning pain that causes my eyes to well with tears.

"Hey..." I hear a soft voice speaking, but a wave of nausea slams into me and I turn my head, spewing vomit. "Shit, call the doctor." A hand presses against the back of my head, smoothing down my hair. "Poppy, can you hear me, sweetheart?"

Forcing my head to cooperate, I ease my gaze toward the unknown person. I take in the woman standing beside the bed I'm occupying. "Where am I?"

She smiles, though seemingly forced, and sighs. "You're in the hospital. Do you remember anything?"

My eyes close as I breathe in, the horror washing over me like a D-list movie on replay. "Bits and pieces... but—" My words cut off as I swallow the acid burning in my throat, willing myself not to puke all over the stranger. "Who are you?"

The door opens, revealing an older man in scrubs. "Miss Jefferson. I'm glad to see you're finally awake."

I stiffen when he lays his hand on my arm, instantly regretting it as pain courses through my bones. The woman, who I don't think is a nurse, moves beside me. "You're safe, Poppy. The doctor just needs to check you over—okay?"

A man I didn't see at first leans against the wall watching me. He starts to move toward me, but my eyes widen at his sudden movement, and my body goes ramrod stiff. He narrows his gaze on me, obviously seeing the change in my demeanor at his approach. The woman turns her head to look at him, giving him a slight shake of her head. "Drake... I think she's a bit frightened by you."

He stops in his tracks, holding his hands out in front of himself. "Hey—Poppy. I'm not going to hurt you. Ah... I'm Gage's brother, and this is Rhiannon. We've been here since last night."

"Gage." My eyes dart around the room, searching for him. "Where's Gage?"

I watch as the woman flicks her eyes toward him, then at the doctor. "Miss Jefferson," the doctor interrupts. "You've been unconscious for the last twenty-four hours. Let's talk about that before you get into anything else, okay?" Nodding my head, because I'm still confused as to how I'm here, I don't push for answers on Gage's whereabouts. "Alright then—you were brought in late last night... unconscious. You were severely dehydrated, but honestly, that was the least of our worries. The previous injury on your flank had been reopened. I've got you on a heavy dose of antibiotics to stem the infection that's begun to fester there and re-sutured the hole. This time, it took fifteen stitches and nine staples to close you up. It will heal, but it won't be pretty, I'm afraid. You've probably noticed the wrap around your waist. Multiple rib fractures are going to make recovery a bit painful. As if that wasn't enough—the head injury you sustained might have some lasting effects, I won't know until the neurologist does another scan. With the other blows you took to your head—" he takes a breath. "I'm surprised the one you took to your temple didn't kill you. You're quite lucky to be alive."

"How–" I pause, taking a deep breath.

"Poppy, you were brought in by ambulance after your friends rescued you from an outbuilding where you were being held. Speaking of which…" He looks toward the man hovering behind the woman. "There is a detective outside waiting to speak with her."

"No. Absolutely not." He moves to the edge of my bed. "Poppy, I promised my brother I'd watch after you, and talking to a detective without our attorney present isn't going to happen."

"I'll let him know she's not ready." The doctor turns back to me. "I'm going to keep you for another day—then Mr. Winston has arranged to move you back to Atlanta, where you'll be monitored by a local doctor."

I don't say anything as he walks out of the room, leaving me alone with Gage's brother and whom I'm assuming, must be Drake's girlfriend, Rhiannon. My eyes pan over to the man who stands watching me with a sympathetic expression. He's wrapped his arm around her protectively as she reaches out and presses her palm against my leg.

"I know you're confused, Poppy. But know that we aren't going anywhere. We're going to be here the entire time, and then we'll take you home."

I nod, finally working up the courage to speak. "Can you tell me where Gage is?"

Drake's lips press together, and I watch a weird emotion skitter across his face. "Nowhere good."

Rhiannon gives Drake a dirty look and rolls her eyes as she clarifies, "Gage is being held without bond for the moment."

"Bond?" My brows knit together in confusion. "Are you saying that Gage is in *prison* right now?"

His brother shares a look with Rhiannon, who simply nods. "Poppy, what's the last thing you remember?"

I close my eyes and take a shaky breath, trying to spark memories I don't want to remember. Visions of Hunter's lifeless eyes and the echo of his cold arm pressed against mine make me gasp. "Hunter. Oh, my God. He's dead because of me."

A sob bubbles from my chest and Rhiannon takes my hand in hers. "Hey—none of that. Hunter is dead because of Alessandro Hugo. *Not* you."

My watery eyes lift to meet her gaze. "And he was furious because of me. If it weren't for me running away, none of this would have happened. I should have just gone back to him and pretended things were fine—or let Archer fake my death."

"We all know things were far from fine. And besides, this was bigger than just you. It may have started there, but how do you think that would have made Gage feel if you'd just disappeared or worse... if he thought you *died*?" Drake steps to the bed. "Because I can tell you how. It would have practically killed him, Poppy. You're the *only* woman my brother has ever loved, aside from our mother. It *crushed* him when she died—it crushed all of us. So no..." He tugs Rhiannon against his frame, tightening his hold on her. "Faking your death would *not* have been the right thing to do."

"I've only brought heartache into his life. And now he's in jail... why is that, Drake?"

A sigh escapes his lips. "Gage was with the men who found you. Archer, my head of security, learned where you were being held. And you know my brother is a bit, well... stubborn. He's how you're here in this bed."

"They arrested him for *saving* me?" I press my hand to my forehead, the pressure building behind my eyes. I don't understand why he would be in trouble for rescuing me.

"Not exactly." Drake mumbles. "Look... Gage wants to be the one to tell you exactly what happened. For now, let's just focus on getting you well. Please know we are doing everything we can to get him out. I won't stop until the local police department relent with their stupid power-trip of wrongly accusing an innocent man of something that was clearly self-defense. But I'm not worried. Alex Whitmire is the best criminal defense attorney I know. And fortunately for us, he can practice here in Alabama."

I cut my eyes at Drake, blinking at the words only halfway register in my brain, "Criminal defense? What was criminal about rescuing me?"

Rhiannon shakes her head with a heavy sigh as she looks up at Drake and murmurs something to him. The pair argue back and forth in hushed words for several moments, most of their whispered conversation impossible for me to understand, though I catch bits and pieces. It's enough to raise my hackles in concern when a couple of keywords reach my ears. The one that makes my stomach sink and a gasp escape my lips is 'life in prison'.

Coughing softly, I murmur, "Life in prison? For *what*?"

Rhiannon and Drake exchange a worried glance with Drake, shaking his head firmly, but Rhiannon gives him a firm look as she turns to look at me, grabbing my hand gently as she sighs. "Poppy, honey… Alessandro is dead…"

25

Gage

To say the last three weeks have been utter hell would be an understatement. I now have a newfound respect for the men and women who work in a prison—seeing as I've now been in one as a resident. The moment I stepped inside the building where Poppy was being held, I knew I wasn't walking out of there the same man.

When I was seventeen, I made a decision that left me a shell of a man before I was even legally considered one. Then Poppy stumbled into my life and changed everything. Pulling the trigger for the second time in my life led me here. But I wouldn't change it for a minute. Even as I sit here staring at the man I'm sharing a cell with. I know without a doubt I'd do it again—without a moment's hesitation. Granted, I'd rather not be in this six-by-eight hell hole, but at least *she's* safe.

Drake visits often, so I know exactly how Poppy is getting along. She's pissed I won't let her come see me but having her visit me *here* would be pure torture. Alex assures me I'll be home free soon—something about the FBI being involved.

His refusing to go with us to the scene pissed me off at first, but it's probably the only reason he can represent me without a conflict of interest now.

"Winston." The sound of my name draws my attention away from my thoughts. Glancing up from my perch on the tiny mattress, I meet the eyes of the block guard. "You're being released. Don't look so thrilled. You'll need to come with me."

"What did you say?" I sit up, certain I heard him wrong.

"You've been granted bond." He steps to the side, glaring at me with an impatient look. "Let's go–unless you'd rather stay."

Popping up from the bed, I bound over to him. "Getting out?"

"Yeah. Seems you've got the attention of some powerful folks and they're not pleased you were denied bond. Friends in high places have its benefits. Let's go–your ride is waiting."

Not giving two shits about leaving behind everything reminding me of my stay here, I follow him out and down the narrow hallway. For the life of me, I can't think of any powerful friends, but I'm not going to complain. I'm practically shoved into a small waiting room and sealed inside. Pacing the floor like a cat on a hot tin roof, I practically jump out of my skin when the door opens again.

"Gage." Alex steps through the opening with a megawatt grin on his face. "Look at you, always the hero... even in jail."

I can't help my eyes from rolling as my head shakes in response. "I'm not a fucking hero. That man was going to die with the way these idiots were just standing around with their thumbs up their asses. Please tell me you've come with good news."

"Yeah, you could call it that. Like I said the last time we chatted… the Feds are involved, and they are pissed at the way those podunk idiots handled this case." I blow out a frustrated breath at the reminder of the cluster fuck it's been, thanks to the small Alabama police department that initially arrested me. Alex had to pull some major strings and call in a bunch of favors to get me transferred to Georgia for my stay in prison. Whoever owed him worked a miracle and got me transferred to the penitentiary here in Atlanta. Alex chuffs a laugh. "Seems that when you eliminate a massive pain in the ass, you can get your slate wiped clean a bit easier. There was a mountain of paperwork, but I was able to get it done and you out this afternoon. Apparently, in a pissing contest, the Feds win every time."

"You're telling me I'm leaving today?" I blink in disbelief. Three weeks in this shithole have felt like a lifetime. Partly because I haven't seen Poppy since finding her on the floor of the metal building of atrocities none of us will ever forget.

"You're being processed out as we speak." Alex smiles and turns toward the door. I watch as he brushes his knuckles across the metal door. "I've got the car waiting outside." The door pushes open, and he turns his head to look at me. "Come on, Trigger. Let's get you home."

Grumbling under my breath at the nickname he's taken to calling me, I follow him through the door and down another hallway. It takes them a few minutes to finish the process, but before I realize it, I'm stepping out into the sunlight a semi-free man.

"I'm parked over here. Drake was going to come, but he felt like you'd want to enjoy the ride without his interference."

"How the hell would he be interfering?" My brow arches in question as we amble across the pavement toward a waiting SUV. I recognize it as one of Archer's, making me glance toward Alex. "Why are you driving Archer's car?"

"Figured you'd want some privacy."

As the words pass his lips, the back door opens and the person I've dreamt about for three long weeks slides out. I vaguely hear Alex chuckle as he rounds the front of the SUV, but I ignore him because the only thing my brain can compute is *her*, the woman taking timid steps toward me. My feet stay planted on the hot asphalt as she stops in front of me. Her eyes are filled with unshed tears as she steps into me and wraps her arms around my middle.

I melt against her as my face burrows into her hair. Her scent assaults me and I can't control the emotion that bubbles out of me as speak her name. *"Poppy."* My palms press her tiny frame into my chest, desperate to pull her closer, but I know she's still recovering from the hell she experienced, so I'm cautious about how hard I squeeze.

She finally breaks the embrace, stepping back slightly to look at me. I can see the remnants of what she endured scattered across her honey colored skin. Light bruises still mar her face along her jaw and hairline, but they aren't the nasty black and blue shade my brother described. From what he told me, Poppy is lucky to be standing here. The fractures to her ribs have finally healed enough that she isn't in constant pain. After several visits with the neurologist, she got the all-clear regarding any lasting damage to her brain—thank God.

"You're here." I press my palm to her cheek. "I was afraid you wouldn't want to see me." Drake mentioned on numerous occasions how angry she was that I wouldn't let her come visit. I did it for her sake, knowing she needed to recuperate —and a small part was because the selfish side of me knew seeing her would be pure torture.

"I've wanted to see you since your brother brought me home... there's no chance in hell I would've missed this moment. Honestly, I worried you wouldn't want me here."

Pressing my forehead against hers, I sigh. "You're all I've thought about for the last three weeks, Poppy. Refusing to let you visit was fucking hell, but I knew seeing you would tear my heart in two. But don't you think for a second I don't want you." I press my lips to hers, pouring every ounce of my feelings for her into the kiss.

"I'm sorry," she says as she pulls her lips away from mine. "I know your stint behind bars is my fault, but no one will really tell me why. Not even the detective would give me a straight answer."

"Let's get in the car. I'll tell you everything you want to know, butterfly." I lace my fingers with hers and guide her to the SUV where Alex has been patiently waiting. Easing her into the backseat, I climb in beside her and pull the door shut. "What do you remember?"

I watch as a myriad of emotions flutter across her face. "Everything—at least until I passed out."

"When we found out what happened, we immediately started digging. It didn't take long to piece it together and then we got information about Hunter—which led us to your location." I take a breath and close my eyes, trying to staunch the memory of seeing her on the ground. "The guys breached the building, and I waited… I wasn't supposed to go inside, but all hell broke loose, and I did it, anyway. My heart stopped beating when I saw you lying there unconscious. I thought you were dead and a part of me died at that moment. Perez was seconds away from being choked to death, so I did the only thing I could. I shot him. I shot Alessandro. He's dead, Poppy. He's gone."

A part of me is expecting her to look at me differently, but when I brave myself to look up, she's staring at me with a look of complete and utter devotion. "Gage." She blinks away the tears slowly seeping from her beautiful hazel orbs and presses her hand against my face. "I hate you had to pull the trigger again—Drake told me how you felt after your parents' deaths. But I'd be lying if I said I wasn't grateful, because I am. You've set me free in the most final way possible and it's like a burden has been lifted from my shoulders. I only regret that you now carry the burden instead."

"There is no burden." Alex's voice cuts through the haze. "I don't mean to interrupt… but you should know this is all going to go away in a few weeks. You'll have to appear in court, but the FBI has made it very clear they aren't pressing charges against you—however…" He adjusts the rearview mirror. "There is a lot of shit to untangle, which means the charges haven't officially been dismissed yet and technically, you're out on bond. So do me a favor and don't skip town." He laughs as he navigates the SUV out onto the highway.

"I have no intention of leaving my house anytime soon. And since I'm jobless, it won't matter."

Poppy cringes beside me, making me tug her against my side. "Don't. I don't give a fuck about the job, Poppy. I don't need it to survive and maybe my brother is right—maybe it's time to join him at Angels' Wings."

She nods against my hold. "I still feel bad they fired you because of me."

"Well... I actually got that overturned as well. You've officially resigned, Gage. In light of the circumstances, I was able to convince the hospital administration to let you resign on paper... so as not to hurt your reputation."

"Alex..." I turn toward him. "I don't know what to say. You've barely taken a break since this mess started and now... *fuck*. What the hell would we do without you?" I rest my head against Poppy. "I feel like I owe you everything. Thanks to you, I get to start forever with her." I inhale her scent, overjoyed to have her in my arms.

Alex's face splits into a massive grin and I can't help but laugh when he wiggles his eyebrows at me in the rearview mirror. "Hey... it's what I do... help get you Winston boys out of the massive shit holes you like to dig. Speaking of, I'll be leaving town this evening to go fix another mess, so I'm serious about you staying put... I've got to go with Archer and try to track down some woman named Izzy, but nobody knows where she went or why. I just got a call this morning, and it seems it's Roland's turn to take a swan dive into the deep end. Why is it you three swore off any serious attachments... but when you get in trouble, it's ALWAYS a woman?"

Roland thought his biggest scar was never having a real childhood... but then *she* happened and nothing prepared him for the the pain loving someone would bring.
https://books2read.com/Bad-Rhythm

Playlist

Maybe—Machine Gun Kelly
For Tonight—-Giveon
911—Ellise
Chaotic—Tate McRae
The Night We Met—Lord Huron
Stay—Rhiannan
I Hate U, I Love U—Garrett Nash
Unsteady—Ambassadors
Like I'm Going To Lose You—Jasmine Thompson
Chasing Cars—Snow Patrol
How To Save A Life—The Fray
Please Don't Go—Joel Adams
You Don't Own Me—Joan Jett
Midnight Sky—Miley Cyrus
S&M—Rhianna
Bad Karma—Miley Cyrus
Little Do You Know—Alex & Sierra
Superficial Love—Ruth B.
A Little To Much—Shawn Mendes

Hold On—Chord Overstreet
One Day—Tate McRae
Wildest Dreams—Madilyn Bailey
I Did Something Bad—Taylor Swift
Follow My Playlist on Spotify @NerdyDirtyBooks

ABOUT

Dori Pulitano

"Welcome to the dark side. We have sexy Mafiosos."

Dori P is the naughtier, much dirtier half of USA Today Bestselling author, LC Taylor. The bad girl Dori embraces her Italian side with heroic hitmen, decadent conflicted dons, and oh so f*ckable assassins trying to trade their devilish ways for salvation and the perfect woman to tie to their bed.

And F**k following the rules... this author is most definitely trigger happy.

Sign up for Dori's newsletter and never miss a new release.
www.authordoripulitano.com

www.ingramcontent.com/pod-product-compliance
Lightning Source LLC
Chambersburg PA
CBHW061207210726
48294CB00006B/1784